BORDERTOWN JUSTICE

Gary McCarthy

LEISURE BOOKS   NEW YORK CITY

To Jeanne Williams
Good friend, fine writer

A LEISURE BOOK®

December 2000

Published by

Dorchester Publishing Co., Inc.
276 Fifth Avenue
New York, NY 10001

If you purchased this book without a cover you should be aware that this book is stolen property. It was reported as "unsold and destroyed" to the publisher and neither the author nor the publisher has received any payment for this "stripped book."

Copyright © 1979 by Gary McCarthy

All rights reserved. No part of this book may be reproduced or transmitted in any form or by any electronic or mechanical means, including photocopying, recording or by any information storage and retrieval system, without the written permission of the publisher, except where permitted by law.

ISBN 0-8439-4811-6

The name "Leisure Books" and the stylized "L" with design are trademarks of Dorchester Publishing Co., Inc.

Printed in the United States of America.

Visit us on the web at www.dorchesterpub.com.

BORDERTOWN JUSTICE

Daybreak found them high above San Diego riding into the hills. Two men silhouetted against the sky. One, tall, broad-shouldered and the other much smaller and bent forward atop a mule. At the crest of a hill they stopped and silently dismounted to watch the sunrise far across the settlement below. They saw the orange brilliance touch the whitewashed adobe walls and creep higher until the tile roofs shone like burnished copper.

The tall one pushed his hat back and wondered when the first rays of sun would burst into Maria Silvas' window and stir her from sleep. Very soon. He pictured Maria's face against the pillow, coal-black hair fanned out beside her head. Before long, he thought, I will ask her to be my wife, and on a morning such as this, I will be there to watch her awaken.

The light hurried across the town and Glen Collins saw the spreading Pacific Ocean, the sailing ships in the port. He took a deep breath and stretched the morning's chill from his muscles. San Diego would be a great city someday. And maybe, if he won the election and became its first sheriff, he could do his part to see that it became the kind of place where folks would stay and raise their families with pride. It would never be a rip-roaring railhead city like Dodge or Abilene. He'd seen those places and they offered no appeal. Those towns would blossom and die before they'd even lived. But here it was different; San Diego was already a hundred years old and founded by Junipero Serra as the Mother Mission of California—San Diego de Alcalá. It had grown very slowly, but now, after a century, what was left was good and Collins knew that it was here he would plant his roots.

But planting roots took money. Maybe Maria didn't understand, but before a man could ask a woman to share his life, he had to have something to offer. The sheriff's job wouldn't pay much, but with his blacksmithing on the side, they could make it.

"You're thinking about her again, ain't you."

He turned, feeling sheepish because Hap Hazard caught him so easily. "Anything wrong with that?"

"Heck no." Hap rolled a cigarette. "No boy, I sure can understand why you stumble around in such a fog. If I was your age and a woman like her showed interest, nothing would have stopped me from marrying and settling in family-like."

"But you never did."

"Nope," he said, looking away. "And maybe I should have. But trapping and hunting buffalo was fun while it lasted. I got no regrets. I just never met a woman like your Maria. And . . . and I reckon, if the truth be known, even if I had, nothing would have come of it. I never cut much of a figure with women. I was always pretty rough around the edges. Wouldn't have been no prize."

Glen Collins shook his head. "I sure don't see what a girl like her sees in me. I got a livery and blacksmith business that barely pays. My clothes are torn and burnt from the forge and I smell like a horse."

"Who says!"

"Well," he admitted. "Once or twice Maria has kind of hinted she wished I'd take a little more care of myself."

Hazard snorted. "She's had the dandies come courting her before. But it's you she favors."

"Maybe . . . maybe the right dandy hasn't come along yet."

"Don't talk such nonsense! If that woman is worth taking she's got to have enough sense to know you're the best catch in San Diego. Hell yes you're poor. But once you become sheriff, things will get better. Even the mayor, Josh Winslow, knows you're the right man for the job. And he's no fool."

"That he's not," Glen agreed. "He's a man I admire."

"Well don't admire him too much. He's got six or seven years on you. There's plenty of time to do as much as him. Right now, though, you just set your sights on winning that election and becoming sheriff. After that, the rest will come easy."

Glen searched the face of the man who had become almost like the father he'd never known. "Do you think I'll win?"

"Sure! The townsfolk aren't blind. You'll make a great sheriff. Do a fine job unless you get shot right off. And that's why we're standing here. Remember?"

"Sure I remember. You never let me forget, Hap. Light's good enough—I might as well start practicing. Go set them up."

Hap Hazard untied a sack from his saddle and slung it across his shoulder. Glen watched him limp away. The old man had tangled with a grizzly bear years earlier in the Big Sur Country up near Monterey. Before he'd emptied his gun, the enraged animal had almost bitten off his leg. That ended his trapping days. Though he'd never complained, Glen knew the leg gave Hap constant pain. There were deep lines around his mouth to prove it. Before he'd ridden the mule into San Diego four years ago, he'd pretty much starved. Glen took him on because he couldn't pay a workingman's wages. It was the smartest move he'd ever made. To begin with, Hap could cook. True it was mostly beans and little meat. But in the first year they'd been together, Glen put on thirty pounds to where his ribs didn't show. Even more important, Hap loved horses and had a way of settling them. More and more, Glen found that they were getting blacksmithing business that no one else in San Diego would touch. Together, they could shoe the wildest horses, horses of Arabian blood owned by the rich Spanish dons.

And now, only a month before the election, Hap was teaching him how to handle a six-gun. Getting elected was going to be easier than staying alive. San Diego wasn't Wichita or Dodge City, but there were gunfights and a sheriff had to be fast or dead.

"Now, boy," Hap called, "these bottles are sittin' here waiting for you to bust. Remember what I've told you. Relax. Try to get your gun out smooth and quick. When it's out, bend at the knees and point. Don't aim. You ain't got time. Just crouch, point, and fire. Six bottles. Don't think about the last bottle you shot. If you ever face more than one man in a saloon shoot-out, your only chance is to start on the fastest, take one shot and go for the next."

"But what if I missed?"

Hap limped down from the hillside. "Boy, if you missed, and he was any good at all, you wouldn't have a thing to worry about. Because if you held up even a split second to follow your first shot, the second man would have the edge and you'd be ventilated. You got to remember this: if some jasper is going to pull a gun, you have to figure he knows how to use it—unless he's drunk. In that case, he'll be slower. Go for his legs if he hasn't cleared leather. You'll have time for two shots before you have to kill."

Glen nodded. He pulled his gun out of the holster and dropped it lightly back down again. He tried to concentrate on all the things Hap said. Bend the knees. Point, don't aim. Go for the second shot, then the third without looking back.

"Ready!"

"Yes."

Hazard lifted his arm. He waited. Twenty heartbeats? Forty? Glen didn't know. He forgot about Maria and the fading sunrise. Suddenly the arm dropped and he was crouching, firing. The roar of his gun boomed again and again. The hammer clicked. Finally. For perhaps three, maybe four seconds, Glen's mind was blank.

The smoke drifted slowly toward the ocean and he straightened. Three out of six. Not good. Not nearly good enough. He shook his head. Someday a gunman would ride into town, and if Glen could do no better, that man would ride out leaving Maria a widow. He pivoted back toward the town and located her house. She would be awake by now, he was sure of it. Glen began to reload. He had to do better.

At mid-morning they stopped. Glen's face was grim as he poked fresh cartridges into the cylinder. "I don't know what it is, Hap. Drawing just doesn't seem to come easy for me. I'm slow, aren't I?"

"No," Hap said frowning, "you're not. But I have to tell you the truth; I don't think you'll ever be real fast."

"I'm not quick. That's what you mean, isn't it."

"Now take it easy, Glen. You're plenty quick. I seen you drop horseshoe nails from your teeth and grab 'em before they hit dirt or the horse knew you'd missed a stroke. No, it's your hands."

"Hands." Glen held them up. "What's wrong with them?"

"Well, to begin with they're suited for holding a hammer, but them fingers are a might thick for dealing cards or handling a six-gun. They're strong hands that are rough-calloused from hard work. You ever see the paws of a card-sharp or a real gunman?"

"No," Glen said.

"Well, I have. Plenty of times. Their hands are soft and they keep care of them like a lady might. That's the reason why they don't go in for fistfighting. They mash a knuckle or break a finger and they're out a business. In the case of a gunman, a broken hand can be terminal."

"I never much thought about it."

Hap winked. "They have. You need to understand that I'm trying to tell you that you'll never have the speed of Hickok or John Wesley Hardin. What we're doing here now is trying to smooth out your draw and sharpen your eye. And that takes time."

"Did you ever get real good with a handgun?" Glen asked.

"Naw. A Sharps rifle was my weapon. A hunter hasn't much use for a pistol. We always wore them in our belts when we came to town. In a saloon, a hunter would more than likely pull a knife than a handgun. But enough time wasted. Let's try a few more bottles. I'll put up three fresh ones."

Glen nodded and took a deep breath. He set his feet, concentrated on the first bottle and tensed. Out of the corner of his eye he saw Hazard's arm drop. Glen stabbed for his gun and felt the handle slap his palm just right. He drew and fired knowing it was as fast as he'd drawn all morning. The gun bucked in his fist six times and he lowered his arm. Smoke drifted down the hillside and Glen smiled. That was much better. Four out of six wasn't bad shooting.

"Hello down there!"

Glen turned. Above him on the grassy slope sat a man on a gray horse. He wore a sombrero, and the silver trappings on his saddle glinted in the sunlight. Glen reloaded and waved the vaquero to approach. The rider prodded the gray forward. The stranger rode erect and Glen saw that he was young and handsome in a dashing sort of way. He wasn't a working cowboy. His clothes were bright-colored reds and yellows. His chaps beautifully tailored, fringed with tanned doeskin. He pulled his horse to a standstill and lightly dismounted.

"I heard the shooting and rode over to investigate. One never knows," he smiled. "Perhaps I might have been fortunate enough to come to the rescue of a beautiful señorita."

"No such luck, I'm afraid." Glen shook his hand. The grip was strong but the hand was uncalloused. He remembered Hazard's comments. Which was this man—gambler or a gunfighter? He didn't look like either. He seemed too young. There wasn't a worry-line on his boyish face and the eyes were bright and friendly.

"My name is Roy," he said.

"I'm Glen Collins. This is my friend Hap Hazard."

Roy nodded. "Pleased to meet you both. And that"—he pointed—"would be San Diego."

"Yes. Welcome to our town. We have the finest people and climate in America. Beautiful isn't it."

"You sound like a mayor," Roy grinned.

"He's practicing," Hazard remarked.

"I see. Does the mayor of San Diego need to be handy with a six-gun?"

"I'm running for sheriff," Glen said, feeling the explanation was adequate.

"A worthy occupation if you are of that breed. Me, I never could see getting shot at for sheriff's pay."

Glen frowned. "It isn't just for the money."

"Oh, of course not. I meant no offense. Sure, someone has to keep the lid on and I admire an honest lawman. But they're hard to find. More often than not they're on somebody's payroll. Why else would a man take the risk?"

Glen shifted uncomfortably. Hap was about to say something but he silenced his friend with a look. "Have you really known that many?"

Roy laughed. "Darn right I have! Sometimes not under the best of circumstances." He motioned toward the bottles. "If you're going to be sheriff you have to realize that shooting at those is one thing—exchanging lead with a man is entirely different."

Glen felt a touch of annoyance. Roy wasn't any older than himself yet talked as though he had all the answers to being a sheriff. "Yes, I guess there is a shade of difference. If I post the law, make it plain to everyone, I hope I'll never have to use a gun."

"You will," Roy smiled. "Of course you will. Ever been in a shoot-out?"

"No."

"I guessed as much. I'm meaning no offense, and you're a big enough man to break up barroom fights; but you can't know how you'll act when it happens."

"I'd do what I had to," Glen said shortly. "Generally you can reason with a person."

"Maybe. Maybe not. I've met a lot of unreasonable men that would empty their six-shooter while you was thinking about what to say."

"You sure seem to know a heap about gunfighting." The tone in Hap Hazard's voice told Glen that he was becoming impatient with the stranger's know-it-all attitude. "Would you be one?"

"A gunfighter?" Laughter bubbled out of Roy's mouth. "No chance! I think a man would have to want an early grave to take up that kind of profession. No siree, I just try to get along with folks. Especially the young ladies," he winked.

There was something about the stranger that Glen didn't like. On the surface he was smooth and easy, but underneath like a deep river churning. Maybe it was the quick-sure way he seemed to come up with an opinion. He was a dandy, though. Glen's eyes dropped to his own clothes. Pants all patched up at the knees and shirt wrinkled and faded. He couldn't help but compare himself to Roy. When he did he felt like a plow horse next to a blooded racing animal. The man's hair was black, his mustache rakish and waxed. Though the day was growing warm, Roy Winslow gave the impression he might never sweat. There wasn't a single girl in San Diego who'd miss him.

"You mind if I made a suggestion?" Roy asked.

"No."

"You're crouching too much. With your knees bent that way it puts a strain on the legs and your whole body is too tense. Forget about bending and try to stay loose. If it helps, knot your fists and squeeze them tight for a couple seconds before you draw. That relaxes your hand and arm muscles. Then, when you bring the gun up, cock it before it clears leather and drop the hammer as it comes level." He turned to face the two unbroken bottles. "When you get to where you can hit them all the time, go for the necks. Makes it more fun."

"Why don't you show us," Hap said.

The almost constant smile faded and Roy nodded quietly. "Don't blink, gentlemen, or you'll miss the show."

Glen didn't blink; there wasn't time. Roy's hand blurred downward and his gun flicked up so swiftly Glen never even saw the barrel clear the holster before the first shot. The second bullet sounded flat with the first. Glen looked at Hap Hazard. The old man whistled softly. "Shaved 'em both."

Roy turned his gun from side to side and studied it for a moment before he spoke. "Glen, how long have you been practicing?"

"Most every morning for six or seven weeks."

"You want to shoot like that, be thinking about six or seven years. An hour every day and no less."

Glen shook his head. There wasn't time enough in his schedule for it. Roy hadn't said as much, but Glen knew the man was a gunfighter whether he admitted it or not. A sense of foreboding crept up his back. He'd never seen anyone shoot that fast. What chance would he, as a new sheriff, have against a man like this? Not much. In fact, none at all.

Roy grinned as if he sensed Glen's thoughts. "Don't worry," he said. "There are probably faster men than me, but not many. You just keep plugging away at those bottles."

"I'll do that and thanks for your help. Maybe I can do something in return. Anything special bringing you to San Diego?"

"The mayor."

"Josh Whitlow?" Glen asked. What would Josh be wanting of this man?

"Yeah, he's my oldest brother."

"I . . . I see." Glen tried to hide his surprise. While there was a facial resemblance, the two brothers were cut from opposite molds. Josh had no flair. Only plenty of good common sense that made people trust him as a banker. He was respectable, perhaps a mite long-winded and boring. The brothers were about the same height, not quite six foot, only Josh was pretty paunchy while Roy was narrow-waisted. Glen wondered what their mayor would think when he saw Roy. Probably, he would disapprove but not likely say anything. It was hard to believe they were brothers.

"I haven't seen Josh for almost five years," Roy was saying. "Oh, a couple of times I've had to ask for some money to get me out of trouble, but what are big brothers for?"

"I wouldn't know. Never had one," Glen said.

"Well, they can come in handy. Me, I've been roaming around for a long time. Spent the last two years chasing the women down in Mexico. Not many got away."

"I don't imagine."

"Why'd you leave Mexico, stranger?" Hazard drawled. "Sounds like you were keeping busy."

He thumbed back his sombrero and Glen saw a muscle twitch in Roy's face as he studied Hazard. Glen broke the silence. "I hope you like San Diego. It's a good, peaceful town."

"Not too peaceful, I hope. Many pretty women?"

"I guess."

Roy laughed. "You guess! Friend you can't be much older than me. What do you do down there, wear blinders? You didn't get married already, did you?"

"Not yet," Glen said evenly.

"Well, I better be riding. I guess we'll probably be running into each other often enough." He grabbed the saddle horn and swung easily up on the gray. "My brother says he's got a good woman. Met her right here in San Diego."

"That's right," Glen said. "Donna is a fine woman and they make a happy couple."

Roy's face softened as he stared down toward town. "I'm real glad to hear that," he said finally. "Josh always did do the right thing. Maybe it's time I started listening instead of talking. He's told me I've got to settle down and sink roots. I think he means to see me running a store and raising kids."

"There are worse things to do. I don't know many men who are happier than your brother. He's made a place for himself down there and folks respect his opinion."

"You sound like him. Know that?"

Glen stiffened. "I thought you said . . ."

"I said I'd listen. That's all. But the way I figure it, there's a lot of country I haven't rode and a lot of pretty women that I haven't kissed. Settling down in one spot with one gal seems like it would be giving up plenty."

"Maybe you just haven't met the right one."

Roy seemed to shake himself from dark thoughts. "Yeah, could be she's waiting for me right down there," he pointed.

Glen felt his stomach tighten. He'd be damned if the finger didn't seem to go directly toward Maria's.

"What's the matter, Collins? I say something wrong?"

Glen shook his head. "Nothing," he mumbled. He turned his back to the horseman and looked at Hap Hazard. "Would you set up some fresh ones? I've got a lot of work to do. More than I realized."

Some time later, Glen stopped and saw the man and gray horse in the distance. A sense of urgency came over him. He had never told Maria Silvas he was waiting to propose when he made sheriff. He didn't have the heart. In the first place she might have turned him down, although he didn't think so. And in the second place she might have accepted; but what if he didn't get elected? Without the sheriff's pay he had no right to ask.

Far below, the sun glinted off Roy's silver *conchos*. Glen jammed fresh shells into his gun impatiently. He thought he'd made his plans. What he'd say to Maria and how much it would take to build their home. He'd even gone so far as to pick names for their first three kids; if she liked them too. Matthew, William, and Travis. They were good names and he'd put a lot of care into choosing each one.

Yeah, he thought unhappily, he'd figured it out except for one thing--that a better man might show up. And Roy was better in the ways that a woman liked. He was even better with a gun.

Glen shoved the Colt down into his holster. He was running out of time.

CHAPTER 2

Glen Collins galloped into town. At Twigg Street he reined in his horse to a walk. The mule and Hap Hazard were not far behind. "Dad-blast it, Glen, what's the hurry!"

"Got a lot of work to do," Glen said.

"Maybe, but you seem as touchy as a teased snake since that Roy Winslow crossed your path."

"Winslow has nothing to do with it."

"I ain't so sure," Hap grumbled. "Why we taking the long way back through town?"

Glen ignored the question.

"You don't have to answer, 'cause I know the reason anyhow."

"All right, you tell me."

Hap swatted the mule until they were riding stirrup to stirrup. "We're going this way because you want to take a peek into the newspaper office and see if that dandy is already talking to Maria."

"That's crazy!" Glen protested. "He's probably visiting Josh."

"Yeah. But you have to make sure."

"It's still a small town," Glen said. "They'll meet sooner or later. I'm not worried."

"The hell you ain't! You have that fella sized up about

the same way as I do. He's a sweet-talking ladies' man and the moment he sees Maria Silvas he'll go after her like bees after honey."

"I got no claim on her," Glen said stubbornly. "Maria is a grown woman and she'll make up her own mind no matter what; I can't change that."

"Well," Hap said, "I agree with part of what you say. She's independent all right. But if I was you, I'd put on a little more of a show. That Roy ain't so fancy you couldn't give him a race."

"I ain't that kind of man and you know it. I can't put on airs, Hap. Now I don't want to talk about it anymore."

"Have it your way, Glen. But Maria is only nineteen and she deserves going after. I got a feeling that, like it or not, you are gonna be forced to put on some of those airs or she'll fall for a dandy like that Roy Winslow feller."

Glen yanked his horse to a standstill. He squeezed the saddle horn until his knuckles whitened. "What am I supposed to do, Hap? Look at me. I'm just a no-frills kind of guy without much to offer. I don't own any fancy clothes and I don't have much money. I've never known a woman like Maria and . . . and when I try and tell her how I feel . . ." He shook his head helplessly. "Well, I just feel like a tongue-tied farmer. I can't get out what's inside me and I've tried. Aw, I don't even know why she bothers."

"You're a fool sometimes," Hap grunted. "But you wouldn't be the first man who found his tongue turned to mush around courtin' time. All I can say is to keep trying. Maria is a woman, but she's got some girl in her too. She probably wants to dance and sing a little before she settles down into the nest."

"I don't know how to dance," Glen said dejectedly.

"Well then, you better learn. Either that or find another girl. Besides, there's other things as important."

"What else?"

"Well," Hap said, scratching his whiskers. "You ain't exactly asking an expert on women, but . . . how about serenading her some night!"

Glen's face took on a stricken appearance. "I can't sing! If the whole town didn't laugh itself silly, they'd arrest me."

"Yeah, maybe that wasn't such a hot idea. What about poetry? Women get real impressed with that."

"They do?" Glen considered the thought. "Maybe I could try it, Hap."

"Sure! And if you can't come up with anything good, we could find some in a book."

"You mean steal someone else's poetry?"

"Why not? She'd never know the difference."

Glen considered Hap's logic. Maybe he could write a few lines of poetry. He'd seen it in the newspaper often enough and some of it was real bad. In fact, Glen had the feeling that most of it was pure nonsense. "Well, Hap, I might give it a whirl. But I wouldn't steal any."

"Have it your way, only you might want to take it by and let the schoolmarm read it over first."

"Nope. My poetry will be for Maria alone," Glen said. The idea appealed to him and all at once he felt better. Maria, he knew, loved writing for the paper and his poetry would impress her. It was a sure-fire idea. He glanced at Hap feeling a great deal of gratitude. "Thanks for the suggestion. Got any more?"

"Well, you play a harmonica about as well as I've ever heard. Does Maria know that?"

Glen shook his head. "She makes me tongue-tied, remember?"

"Hell-fire, boy! Play her a tune once in a while. Something romantic."

"It's easy for you to say, Hap. You don't have to do it.

What am I supposed to do, just walk up and start blowing away?"

"You are the most thickheaded blacksmith I've ever known! All you have to do is just mention that you make up great songs late at night when you're thinking of her. Songs of love. Then you play 'em on the harmonica." Hap winked. "That'll really grab her by the heart. She'll beg you to play 'em. Naturally, then it's up to you to get the tongue unstuck and not botch the music up."

"You're a genius, Hap!" Glen reached over and slapped him on the back. "Just think, me, a poet and a man who creates beautiful love songs."

"It's gonna be impressive all right." A grimace replaced the smile on Hap's lips. "Don't look now, but we got trouble riding this way."

Glen saw them almost at the same time. The image of Maria's eyes shining with admiration while he read poetry and created music vanished. Chase Lawson and four of Howard Trimmer's cowboys were approaching from the far end of the street. A tight fist of anger balled up in Glen's stomach. Chase was in the middle surrounded as always by his hard-cased cronies. This was the man he had to beat in the coming election and there was an open understanding between them it might come down to a gunfight.

He saw Chase stiffen in his saddle. His big florid face twisted with hate. The distance closed steadily. The fact that his opponent for sheriff was taking money and orders from the wealthiest rancher in San Diego County didn't seem to matter to most folks. Maybe it was because Chase spent every day in the saloons buying drinks and slapping backs.

Yeah, Chase was buying votes, and in the background, Glen hadn't a single doubt that Howard Trimmer was pulling strings and applying his enormous financial pressure. If Trimmer could intimidate enough of his neighboring ranchers to have their crews vote for Chase, the election was lost. Between the pair, Glen knew enough money was being loaned to put a dent in the local banking business. That was straight from Josh Winslow. Yes, friends and supporters of Chase Lawson for sheriff—no-interest loans—you pay with your vote.

At ten yards, Chase reined in. "Well," he said with a rigid grin, "what do we have here? Young Glen Collins and his crippled friend returning from the morning's hunt. What did you shoot today? Beer or whiskey bottles?"

The five men brayed with laughter. "Any of those mean ole bottles shoot back?" Chase cackled, his big shoulders shaking with mirth.

Glen held his silence for a moment. His right hand dropped to his thigh and he clenched a fist. When he opened it, the fingers were relaxed. "Not today," he said when the laughter died. "How about you? How many votes do you plan to buy this afternoon? Trimmer gave his boy some spending money, huh?"

The grin on Chase's face dissolved like grease in a frying pan. The man's nostrils flared and his voice went flat and hard. "You accusing me of something?"

"Maybe."

Beside him, Hap chuckled. "Maybe we both are, mister. What of it?"

Out of the corner of his eye Glen saw the long buffalo rifle. It was rested across Hap's saddle and was pointed in the general direction of Chase Lawson. The way the old hunter had it positioned, Glen knew he could twist and fire faster than Chase could blink. There was only one bullet but it was like a cannonball; nothing it struck could hope to survive.

Chase eyed the rifle and Glen saw him swallow. He began to hedge. "You got no proof to say that."

Glen smiled. It was obvious that Chase wasn't going to get foolish. "I guess you're right. Only a man can't help knowing what he sees and hears."

"Oh yeah! What's that supposed to mean?"

"Means you're bought, wrapped, and paid for."

He said it slowly and his fingers twitched near his gun. Lawson was known for his temper. If he lost all reason, Glen knew he was going to have to do some shooting. Hap might get Chase, but the other four would come hard. Out of the corner of his eye, Glen saw a movement. He realized it was Robert Stewart. The man was oblivious to everything.

"Glen! Thank heavens you're back! I've got a problem."

The appearance of Stewart defused Chase. With a grunt of disgust he spurred his horse past. But the look in his eye was murderous and Glen knew their gunfight was that much closer. He directed his attention back to Stewart, not sure if he was grateful for his arrival or not. Glen straightened in the saddle and forced a smile. "Howdy, Mr. Stewart, what can I do for you?"

"Milly's sister came down sick in Los Angeles. Just got a letter and we have to go. I need my horses shod—now—so we can leave at daybreak." Stewart wrung his bony hands together. He looked as if he were going to cry. "I hate to take the time off. You know that road. Two days' hard travel each way, but Milly is close to her sister. I'd never hear the end of it if Cora is really sick. I mean if she should die. That's why we have to leave in the morning."

Glen reined his horse past the newspaper office. Stewart seemed about to come unhinged with worry. "Take it easy. I'll have your horses ready."

"Thanks! Knew I could count on your help." He hesitated. "I'm a little concerned about the rear axle on our carriage. Suppose you could take a look at the thing?

Maybe it just needs grease. You know I'm no good with manual tasks."

"We all have our talents, Mr. Stewart. I wouldn't be much at keeping books the way you do."

The compliment wasn't missed and Stewart actually smiled. "Well, that's kind. Anytime you want me to set up a ledger system for the Blackhawk Livery Stable maybe we can trade services."

"That'd be fine," Glen said. "I'm hoping my business will get big enough that I can't keep track of it in my head."

"A good set of records, young man, will pay for itself many times over. It can show you where to cut expenses, slice away the fat."

"There ain't no fat," Hap Hazard grunted. "If there was, me and Glen would eat it with our beans." He chuckled, obviously pleased with himself.

The bookkeeper frowned; he wasn't amused. "There's always a little money wasted in every operation. I showed the American Hotel how to reduce their expenditures on soap." He cleared his throat, wanting absolute attention. "By slicing the bars into quarters, they will save about . . . about a dollar ten a month. A small savings, I admit, but all the same a savings. Just like dropping pennies in a piggy bank each morning."

Glen chuckled in a way he hoped would indicate he was impressed. The way some of those freighters and cowboys rode in, he figured they'd just about get their hands clean.

"A quarter bar of soap?" Hap gulped. "Well if that ain't . . . why that wouldn't properly suds up a frog!"

"Mr. Hazard, I know different," Stewart protested with annoyance. "Before I made the suggestion, I personally bathed using that amount. I trust you would be honest enough to admit I am clean."

"Can't tell," Hap grunted. "Wind is blowing your direction."

Glen smiled weakly. Mr. Stewart was a customer and a very unhappy one. "Hap is only joking," he said. "And we'd better be getting to those horses of yours. See you later."

At La Casa de Estudillo, they turned right. This was the most beautiful residence in San Diego. Whitewashed adobe walls surrounded the house and courtyard. Inside, it was always cool because Jose Antonio had made the roof tiles thick and planted many trees. Glen often visited Señora Maria Victoria Estudillo. The old lady was a gracious hostess and they enjoyed each other's company. On hot days, Glen knew she could always be found in the courtyard by the fountain.

Maria Estudillo was lonely. Her late husband had been distinguished and Glen listened to her talk of him with pride and love. Jose Antonio was both treasurer and mayor of San Diego before his death at only forty-seven. But he left much and was well remembered.

As they rode by the great house, Señora Estudillo herself appeared. Glen smiled with genuine affection at the Spanish lady. Both he and Hap tipped their hats. "Good afternoon."

"Señor Glen, Señor Hazard," she replied looking up at him with her penetrating black eyes. "I have a surprise for you. Something to say."

"Always a pleasure to listen, señora."

"I will hold a fiesta in two weeks' time. And," she said, bobbing her head with measured excitement, "there will be dancing in the courtyard and much playing of guitars. There will be wine and lovely ladies. A great celebration and I wish to invite you, my friends, before all the others."

"You flatter us with the honor," Glen said gravely.

Her nose wrinkled. "There is a price. You must both dance with me!"

They laughed and Hap said, "With pleasure and more than once, I hope."

"If you wish, Señor Hazard."

"We both wish, señora."

"Good. Even an old lady does not like to appear undesirable. But I tell you now so that you, Glen, can have first chance to ask Maria Silvas. I want to see you dance with her. It will bring back the memory of how Jose Antonio and I danced on our wedding night."

She was quiet for a moment. "It will be fifty years."

Glen dismounted. "It is known that you and Jose Antonio were the handsomest couple ever to be wed in California."

"Perhaps," she said softly. "But that was long ago and this is now." She straightened. "Go, for I understand you must have work to do."

Glen nodded, then impulsively kissed her on the cheek. Her eyes sparkled mischievously. "You are bold, señor, like Jose Antonio. Now, like then, I will scold and say 'Get to work.'"

"Perhaps that is why he accomplished so much, señora," Glen said, getting back on his horse.

"I did not always say that. If I had, he would have done even more." She turned and promenaded back to the house.

"Some woman," Hap chuckled.

"The best." Glen prodded his horse forward until they rode into his Blackhawk Stable. There was work to begin.

They unsaddled and set the horses loose in his pole corral. Glen strode quickly into the barn and climbed a ladder to the hayloft. At the west end overlooking the street, he'd built a sleeping room for himself and Hap. Together, they'd agreed on one luxury, a large window that faced the San Diego harbor. In the evening, there were spectacular sunsets on the ocean. He and Hap always seemed to find themselves up in the room in time to see the sun slip into the water. Someday, he wanted Maria Silvas to stand beside him and witness the sight.

He unbuckled his gunbelt and placed it under the bed. Then he climbed back down to the shop, retrieved his leather blacksmith's apron from a wall peg and tied it to his waist. He felt more accustomed to the apron than the Colt revolver. Maybe that should tell him something. If only he could shoot like Roy Winslow!

How fast, he wondered, was Chase Lawson? Probably faster than himself. He'd be finding out soon enough, of that there wasn't much doubt.

Maria Silvas left the newspaper office at six o'clock. She was tired but her step was quick and light. Mostly, it was because she enjoyed her work. She was responsible for both soliciting new advertising and reporting. Though her looks and charm made it easy to increase the advertising, she much preferred writing copy. But there was never enough time or space to put everything into print.

San Diego was bustling with activity—streets were being surveyed, mines flourished and went bust. In the harbor, sailing ships brought visitors and supplies from all over the world. And from the rolling hillsides to the east, they received a rich cargo fresh from San Diego's orchards and vineyards. Everywhere Maria turned, there were exciting stories and her large and almond-colored eyes missed very little.

A half block from the newspaper office she stepped inside her father's saddle shop. Juan Francisco was stooped over his workbench carving intricate floral patterns on a stirrup leather. Maria peered over his shoulder. "Father, it is time to rest. You should come home now. You must eat."

Juan laid down his knife and studied the work. "Is it not beautiful," he said, running his brown hands caressingly over the leather.

"Yes it is, but . . ."

"This saddle gives me more pleasure than any I have ever made. It is for Señor Taylor. He is very wealthy and a fine man too. He wants me to decorate it with silver. I have always wished to do a work such as this."

"How much would it cost, father?"

"I am not sure. Señor Taylor himself will bring the silver to my shop when all is ready. He has commissioned the best silversmith in San Diego to do the work. But it is up to me to put the leather and metal together in marriage."

She passed her fingers across his thin shoulders. He wouldn't leave his work until very late. And before dawn, he would return to the shop. He worked too hard. Maria felt a touch of anger. Señor Taylor had done without such a saddle all his life. What then was the hurry? Could not her father have normal rest?

"Don't worry, Maria," Juan said, turning to her, "I will not stay late. Good night."

"Good night, Father."

Maria stopped at Wallach's Store and bought potatoes and flour. Since her mother died, she had taken over the responsibility of caring for Juan. When he returned late tonight, she would hear him and rise to cook his meal. Maria knew that he would protest, but in the end, eat. Her father was a good man, but when it came to his health, he had no sense at all.

Far up San Diego Street, Maria heard the striking of a hammer on an anvil. She stopped for a moment to listen, knowing Glen Collins was hard at work. The sound had a rhythm. It was strong and sure like the man. But, like the man, the iron he forged seemed to Maria to be too hard and brittle. The horseshoes he made always looked the same, functional but colorless. If she could only get Glen to open up and laugh with her. She'd been seeing him for almost a year, and during that time, there had been moments when she almost loved him. Could not he show a little more ardor? Were there fires deep inside Glen Collins that glowed as hot as his forge? Maria hoped with all her heart there were.

On impulse, she decided to see him. Rounding the corner at Couts Street, she almost bumped into a man. For a moment, as their eyes met, Maria felt the potatoes and flour grow heavy in her hand. He was extraordinarily handsome. He bowed as she passed and she knew his eyes were on her.

The anvil sounds rang louder in her ears. Maria kept walking. She hoped the stranger did not follow, but at least it would have been interesting to see how Glen Collins would react. Maybe, she thought, it was time to stoke the fire in his heart. And if that fire only smoldered, perhaps it was best to discover it soon.

CHAPTER 3

Glen Collins held the horseshoe up with a pair of tongs and studied it carefully. He placed his blacksmith hammer on top of the anvil and dashed the glowing shoe in a nearby bucket of water. There was a sizzle and a cloud of acrid smoke rose into the air. He waited five seconds for the metal to cool and inspected it critically. "I think she's just right now, Hap."

"Well tack her down and file the hoof smooth," Hap said, scratching the sorrel and keeping her relaxed. "We still got one more front to finish."

"Don't worry, Hap, the last one goes fastest."

"Well, I hope so," the old man grumbled. "Otherwise, we're likely to be working until midnight."

"These horses' feet are in bad shape. Stewart lets them go too long and one of these days his animals will go lame. But not this time. I don't care much for Stewart but Milly is nice. I'd feel bad if they didn't get up to Los Angeles in time because I hurried and did a poor job. It's a matter of pride to me."

"Just like my father," Maria said, appearing in the entrance of the barn. "He also works very slowly but with great pride. That is why he is the best at his trade. Like you are, Glen Collins!"

He tossed the shoe back into the water bucket.

"Maria." He absently brushed his hands down his shirt front and slapped dust from his pants. "I'm . . . I'm real happy to see you."

Hap said something unintelligible and Glen saw a grimace on his face. The meaning was clear enough. His greeting sounded like a schoolboy. Stiff and unpolished. Glen cleared his throat. "Maria, you enter this livery like a pretty flower springing out of a manure pile!"

There was a sudden fit of coughing from Hap. Before Glen could move, the old man dropped the halter and scuttled out the door. Glen's heart sank. Sheepishly, he glanced at Maria. She was shaking with barely controlled laughter. Glen flushed with embarrassment. "Uh, how's your father today?"

She took a deep breath, seemed to gain control. "He is fine. Very excited over the saddle he is creating for Señor Taylor." She paused. "Glen, do you really think of me as a pretty flower?"

"Ah . . . yeah, Maria, I do." He fished the horseshoe from the water bucket, trying to think of something elegant to say. His mind was a blank.

"That is very sweet of you."

"It's the truth," he mumbled. "I wonder where Hap rushed off?"

"Would you like me to hold the sorrel?"

"If it wouldn't be too much trouble."

"Of course not. You know I love horses. Just like you do. Perhaps we could go for a ride in the hills together some day soon."

"I'd like that!" He bent down and picked up the hoof, then placed the shoe. He pulled nails from his pocket and stuck them between his lips and took his hammer from a leather loop at his belt. One by one, with quick accurate blows, he drove the nails cleanly into the hoof. It took all of his concentration for he felt Maria studying him.

The horse was growing tired of standing on three legs. Suddenly, Glen felt its weight shift and he grabbed the hoof with both hands.

"Easy, easy," Maria crooned. "It is almost done." She bent over and picked up his hammer from the dirt. The horse quieted. Maria's face was very close.

"Thanks," he said, forgetting the nails protruding from his lips. They dropped on his apron and slid to the ground. Inwardly, Glen cursed himself for being so clumsy. Hadn't Maria just told him that he was a fine blacksmith? He sure wasn't acting like one dropping the hammer and then the horseshoe nails like a greenhorn. Now she probably thought he was as clumsy with his hands as he was with words. Could he do nothing right in her eyes?

"Here are your nails, Glen. Do you lose many?" she teased.

"Only when you're around, Maria. Do you think," he hesitated, his finger traced around the edges of the horseshoe, "do you find me amusing?" There, it was out.

Maria looked deep into his eyes. There was nothing amusing at all the way she seemed to read his thoughts. "There are times, like this, that I think you are funny. It is when I enjoy you most."

"I don't want to be laughed at, Maria. And I don't try to be funny."

She placed a hand on his sleeve. "I've hurt your feelings. I should never laugh at you again. I am sorry. But it is because you make me laugh sometimes that I like you. Can you understand?"

"I'm not sure," he said honestly.

He drove the final nails home and shaped the hoof. When he stood, she came up to his shoulders. Most girls didn't. Maria was at least five eight. He wanted to touch her, but as he lifted his big hand he saw it was blackened from the fire and dirt. He dropped it to his side. "Maria, the way you feel is important to me. I . . ."

"How's my horses coming along? Almost finished?" Stewart called, popping his head around the corner. "Oh, good evening, Maria. I hope you're not holding Glen up any."

Maria blinked. "I will try not to, Señor Stewart."

"Just kidding," he said. "I wish I had me a pretty helper like that."

Glen tried to be civil. "Once in a while I get lucky."

"Well, I hope you get lucky enough to win the election. Chase Lawson is doing a lot of politicking down at the saloons every night. You know, he does have experience. Five years as a lawman in Colorado."

"Did anyone ever think to ask why Chase left?"

Stewart scratched his jaw. "I believe he said he just got itchy feet. Probably wearied of all that snow."

"Sure," Glen said drily.

"Well I don't see that's the issue," Stewart pressed. "The plain fact is that Chase Lawson knows the job and you don't."

"Maybe he knows it wrong!" Glen picked up the tongs and snatched a shoe from the forge. He beat it into a half-moon, sparks flying.

Stewart seemed to realize he'd said too much. He inched forward, eyes wary. "Don't misunderstand me, Glen. I'll support you same as Milly. I'd just hate to see this town lose a good blacksmith . . . I mean sheriff in a one-sided gunfight."

"That's my problem, Mr. Stewart. I know the risks and I figure I can handle the job. Better than Chase Lawson by a long shot."

"I hope so. Milly told me that very same thing. But you're pretty easygoing, Glen. Maybe some folks won't take you serious."

Glen struck the shoe so hard it almost formed a circle. "Maybe those same folks are in for a surprise!"

"Sure. Sure," Stewart said, backing away. "I know you've been riding out every morning to practice with a gun. We can hear the shots from my house. Even Chase has spoken of it."

"Oh yeah? What does he say?"

Stewart glanced at Maria, his eyes searching for help. She looked away and Stewart pulled a handkerchief from his rear pocket. "My," he gulped, "it gets hot in here. Must be the forge." He mopped his face. "I better get back and help Milly. Let you get on with your work."

"Appreciate that," Glen snapped. He returned his attention to the horseshoe. It was misshapen. He stabbed it back into the fire, then began pumping the billows furiously.

Her fingers brushed his shoulder. "Glen, do not let that man make you angry. He is not mean, only foolish with his words."

He stopped pumping the billows. The glow from the forge made Maria's face glow and her black hair shine. It was as if she were standing on a mountain with a whole sunset radiating upon her. He almost told her that, but remembering his first try at being poetic he decided to wait. "I guess you're right," he said, relaxing. "It's just that Stewart is always saying the wrong thing."

"Then do not listen." She turned back to the sorrel. "Let me help you finish with the last shoe and then I must go."

"Maria, have you heard the things that Chase Lawson is saying about me? You must have. You talk to people all day long."

She hesitated. "He is a braggart and Howard Trimmer is giving him money."

"Yes, I know. Others have told me how Chase is spending every night going from one saloon to the next buying drinks."

"That's true." Maria frowned. "I don't understand how men can let themselves be bought that way. Or women either."

"Women?" Glen frowned. "How's he buying them?"

"Oh, in little ways. I saw him at Manasse and Company the other afternoon. He was bowing to all the ladies and giving peppermint sticks to their children."

Glen expelled a deep breath and shook his head in dismay. "I don't know what to do, Maria. Chase is being backed by Trimmer and it's as clear to me as the nose on my face. The man owns half the grazing land in the North County; now he wants a stranglehold on the town. I guess he figures if he has the sheriff in his pocket, he's off to a good start."

"Is he that bad?"

Glen shrugged. "Depends on who you ask. The way I hear it, Trimmer figures everyone is an enemy unless they come around to his way of thinking. I've had riders come by and tell me he controls that range up there like a king. Anyone crosses his land without permission, they're in trouble."

Maria was quiet for a minute. She drew a circle in the dirt with her shoe, then seemed to make a decision. "Glen, why are you running for sheriff? Is your business so poor?"

Glen looked away. Should he tell her? He wasn't totally sure himself. Yes, there was the money and a chance to marry this girl. But there were other reasons too. San Diego was his city and it had a right to an honest sheriff who owed no one. The idea of Chase Lawson running things the way Trimmer wanted was plain wrong. Someone had to stand up and enforce the laws for everyone. Justly and without favoritism or strings. Yes, he felt an obligation to San Diego he meant to pay, but deep inside he was doing it for Maria. He faced her squarely. "I'm surprised you haven't guessed."

Maria straightened and seemed to grow taller. "I think I know. It's just that I want to hear you tell me."

"All right," he said, "it's time you knew."

"Hello in there!" a voice called.

Glen whirled around and there was Roy Winslow. "Damn," he swore softly.

"Well hello, Glen," Roy said smiling broadly and gazing at Maria. "I sure hope I'm not interrupting anything."

There was a long moment of silence as Glen fought to control his feelings. Roy was interrupting and knew it.

Roy doffed his sombrero and bowed to Maria with the deepest respect. "Ah, we meet again!"

"What do you want?" Glen said angrily.

Roy almost looked hurt. "It's my horse; he is worn out from so many miles." His black eyes danced at Maria. "I wish I could tell the animal my thanks for bringing me to this place so that I might look upon one so beautiful as you, señorita."

"You could go over to Seeley's Stable," Glen said stubbornly. "It's a little closer to the hotel and might be more convenient."

"Well that's real kind of you," Roy drawled. He was smiling again, so sure of himself. "But this seems just fine to me. Besides, I can see that you might need the business. And I always try to help the underdog."

Glen stood thunderstruck, the veiled insult so casually delivered. At his sides, his fists knotted.

"Glen," Maria said quickly, "perhaps we should be introduced. The horse does look weary."

"Well thank you, señorita! My name is Roy Winslow and I am honored to meet one so fair."

"I am Maria Silvas," she said gravely. "Where do you come from?"

The smile almost slipped and Glen saw Roy's eyes blink twice before answering.

"Oh," he shrugged, "just about any place you name. In truth, Señorita Silvas, I have to confess to being sort of footloose. As soon as I get settled I get the urge to move on. I guess I'm a little too wild to tame."

"I understand," Maria said. "Are you related to our mayor, Josh Winslow?"

"Yes. Josh is my oldest brother. He's been after me for years to come to San Diego." Roy winked. "I'm glad I finally did."

"I hope," Glen said, "you'll be enjoying your stay even if it is short."

"Oh I didn't say it would be short," Roy chuckled. "This time I'm really going to make an honest attempt at putting down roots. Josh figures to help me get established here."

Maria smiled. "Your brother is very popular. It must have been a happy reunion."

"It will be, señorita."

"Then you haven't seen him yet?" Glen asked. "I saw you ride into town. You've been here all afternoon."

"That's true. I'm glad to know you're keeping track. The fact is, I didn't want to interrupt him during business hours. There will be plenty of time for getting reacquainted."

It was Glen's turn to smile. "Well, I wouldn't worry about that. Besides, the bank closes at five and that was more than an hour ago."

"Really. I guess I've been captivated by your town and lost track. But now, how about my horse?"

"I'll put him up. Two bits a day."

Mr. Stewart appeared. "Glen, I been studying that

axle. It's got me worried. Would you come on over and have a look before it gets too dark. Boy," he said, "Milly sure is in a stew to get out first thing in the morning. I don't know what we'll do if the axle can't be fixed."

"Don't fret," Glen said. "If I have to work all night I'll have it ready."

A flood of relief washed across Stewart's cadaverous face. "I sure thank you. I know that don't take the place of hard money for working this late, but thanks all the same."

"Forget it." Glen looked to Maria. "I'll walk you home."

"That is kind, Glen, but it would be out of your way to Señor Stewart's; the light is almost gone."

Roy bounced forward. "I'll accompany you with pleasure, señorita!"

"Thank you," she said, "it is only a short way."

Roy beamed. "Don't forget my horse. I'll leave him right here."

"Do that." Glen searched Maria's face. "I'll be seeing you," he whispered.

"I'll look forward to it, Glen." She stepped up close. "Please don't work too late. You look tired tonight and worried."

Glen seethed as Roy and Maria walked away. They were talking and he wondered what they found to discuss so soon. Hell, he couldn't even think of things to say to her half the time. He spun on his heel, unable to watch any longer. "Come on, Stewart," he said roughly. "Let's take a look at that damned axle."

As they strolled toward her house, Maria Silvas felt an unexplainable gaiety. Beside her, Roy Winslow carried the potatoes and flour. He had a jaunty air and talked with great animation about the sights he'd visited in Mexico.

But surprisingly, Maria only half listened. Her mind was awhirl with the memory of Glen Collins. Usually so calm and sure, he had, she thought, almost shown her something new inside. And the look she had received. There had been love and passion in those eyes and she was moved. A slow smile touched her lips and Roy, seeing it, talked even faster. Glen was jealous!

She glanced sideways at the young man beside her. For the first time she noticed that people stopped to watch them. She felt a surge of pride and her smile widened. Perhaps the arrival of Roy Winslow was a godsend. At least it would enliven things.

"Maria?"

She turned, shaken out of her thoughts.

"Usually," Roy said, "women listen to me when I speak."

"I'm sorry," she answered. "It was very unkind of me. What were you saying?"

He nodded with understanding. "It was not that important. I was only asking if you and Glen Collins were to be married."

"Married?" She laughed. "That is for the future to say. He has not asked."

"No disrespect, señorita, but he is a foolish man."

"He is not foolish! He is very sensible and works too hard. Perhaps he has not had time."

"I find that hard to believe."

Maria felt a flash of anger. Who was this man who so boldly questioned, then did not accept? "Señor Winslow, you do not understand Glen. Next month he faces an election for our sheriff. In the afternoons and often late at night he works. In the morning he and his friend, Señor Hazard, go up into the hills and practice with guns."

"Yes, I met them. He told me he wanted to be sheriff."

Roy shook his head discouragingly. "I think he should stick to the livery business."

"Why do you say that?" she challenged.

Roy stepped in front of her, blocking the boardwalk. "Please do not misunderstand. I'm sure he'd make a fine sheriff if he lived long enough."

Maria shivered. Her mouth suddenly went dry. "What are you saying?" she whispered.

Roy took her arm. "Maria, I'm sorry. I meant nothing. You look pale. Are you all right?"

She shook her arm free. "Of course, only why did you say that? Have you heard about trouble Glen should know? Is Chase Lawson . . ."

"It's nothing like that, Maria. But I saw him shooting at bottles this morning and he isn't fast."

She relaxed. "Oh, is that all? For a moment you frightened me."

Roy stepped back and leaned up against a building. His eyes were very thoughtful. "I didn't realize you would be so upset. But listen, Maria. A lawman has to be quick on the draw. Most often it's enough just having people know you're fast. Then they won't be so likely to issue a challenge. Even drunk they'll think twice. But Glen seems to me like just an easygoing nice guy."

"What you seem to be saying, Señor Winslow, is that Glen has not had to draw his gun and kill another. Do I understand you?"

"Well . . . well I wouldn't quite put it that way, but yes."

Maria's eyes flashed. "Then I agree with you. He should not be sheriff for that is a high price to pay, the taking of another's life." She suddenly changed the line of discussion. "I would gather, by the way you talk and wear your gun, that you have paid such a price."

He whistled softly. "I'm really sorry I even brought the

whole thing up. Listen," he said, with a pleading voice, "can't we drop the subject and talk about something else?

"Let me tell you about the great cities I have seen and what the ladies wear." He grinned. "But I must start by confessing you are the most beautiful woman I have ever laid these sad eyes upon."

She was completely disarmed. Perhaps she had been too quick to take offense. Besides, she really did want to hear about the clothing fashions in other places. She stepped around him and started walking. He fell in beside her. "Well?"

"Oh yes. Now to begin with, the wealthy señoras in Mexico City . . ."

It was much later. They'd been standing at her door for a long time but Maria was not anxious to go inside. Roy Winslow seemed to know more about women's fashion than anyone she'd ever known. In the past hour she'd learned about the styles being worn all the way from Mexico to San Francisco to New York. Maria listened intently now for she would write the story for the *San Diego Union.* She questioned Roy closely until he finished.

"Maria, this food is getting heavy. Can I carry it inside for you?"

The interview, she sadly concluded, was over. "I think not. I'm sorry I hadn't noticed the package you carried for me. I was so fascinated by what you were saying."

"There's more," he said quickly. "Let's just go inside and I'll put these down for you. Then I'll tell you about what I saw a great opera singer in Virginia City wearing only this spring."

"I'd like to hear about it," she said truthfully. "But another time. I must go inside now and prepare food for my father. He may be home any time."

"Oh. Well, yes, I suppose you must," Roy said, disappointment in his handsome face. "Will I see you tomorrow?"

"I'm sure you will. San Diego is still a small town. If you are going to stay we will run into each other often."

"I sincerely hope not always by chance."

Maria studied the face and felt her own cheeks grow warm. "We shall see," she whispered. Then she darted inside and closed the door.

CHAPTER 4

The axle on Stewart's carriage was not broken and Glen sighed with relief. He greased the wheels and tightened the carriage bolts. Then he returned to his livery and helped Hap feed and water the livestock. It was almost nine o'clock before he finished Stewart's second horse and led it back to the bookkeeper's house.

"You're all ready to go," he said wearily.

Stewart nodded. "I sure thank you, Glen. Milly is grateful for you helping get us ready."

"Happy to do it." Glen waited and the silence grew.

"Oh," Stewart said finally, "I reckon you want your pay." He reached into his pocket and pulled out money. "How much was that again?"

Glen held out his hand. "Two dollars and thirty-five cents," he said evenly.

"My, I guess it was your lucky day."

He thought about Roy Winslow and Maria Silvas. Lucky, hell! The day had started downhill from the moment Winslow rode into view. He hadn't been able to keep his mind off them since Roy had walked her home.

Glen waited while Stewart counted the money twice. It was common knowledge that the stingiest man in San Diego also had one of the largest bank accounts at Josh Winslow's. It was no small wonder.

"Here you go, young man."

"Thanks."

"You should count it, Glen. Of course I wouldn't cheat you but I might have made a mistake." He chuckled. "Even a bookkeeper has been known to do that."

"I'll take the chance," Glen replied. "Good night Mr. Stewart, and have a safe trip."

On the way back to the stable he veered around the plaza and passed Maria's house. The shades were drawn but a lamp glowed from inside. Glen stood watching a long time until the light blinked out.

On the west side of the plaza a half block up San Diego Avenue, he could hear the tinkling of a piano interspersed with laughter. That would be the Blue Beard Saloon. There were several others Glen preferred as a place to relax but the Blue Beard definitely drew the most business. The thought struck him that Chase Lawson and some of Howard Trimmer's cowboys would probably be there tonight buying drinks. A slow smile crossed his lips. "I wonder if Chase would buy me one?" he asked aloud.

No matter, he had Stewart's money in his jeans and he felt mad enough to court trouble if Chase was foolish enough to crowd him.

Glen headed toward the saloon with a resolute set to his jaw. Besides, he wasn't wearing a gun and maybe that was best. If Chase got rough Glen figured he could handle any truck that came his way with fists. He was going to have a drink on Howard Trimmer even if he had to ask for one.

The Blue Beard was a big saloon and its first owner had painted the inside blue with a white ceiling. Behind a long mahogany bar there were pictures of sailing ships and one of a shipwreck. The ship was diving for the bottom, its masts almost flat to the water. Right out in front, five men in a rowboat pulled to get away. The sea was high and Glen could almost taste the fear of death from the men's faces. One sailor was standing and pointing to a great wave which was about to smash their boat to kindling wood. Everytime Glen walked into the saloon his eyes were drawn to that picture.

He pushed through the doors and stopped for a moment to look at the shipwreck. Then he shook his head at the pity of all men who'd ever gone down at sea. "Whiskey," he said, bellying up to the bar.

The bartender was a man he'd seen before around town but did not know. Glen took his drink and twisted around with his back to the rail. The whiskey tasted good and he laid an empty glass down. "I'll have another."

Chase Lawson was playing cards toward the back of the saloon. Glen recognized him by the broad shoulders and the rattlesnake band he wore around his stetson. The man was seated with his back toward Glen with three cowboys that figured to be on Trimmer's payroll. Glen took his second whiskey and sipped it slowly. He nodded to several men he knew and shook hands with a couple others. Several minutes passed before Chase seemed to get the word that his opposition stood waiting. His big head swiveled around and Glen was again reminded that Chase was a mighty tough-looking hombre. He was shorter than Glen by a good three inches but beefy. Chase's nose was flat from being busted so many times; that didn't make Glen feel any easier because his knuckles were also flat from hitting a lot of folks. Two years earlier, Chase had gotten drunk and beat the hell out of three drifters in this very bar. Now he was running for sheriff. Folks had mighty short memories sometimes.

Glen saw Chase lean forward across the table and the three Trimmer cowhands listened intently. Their heads nodded and suddenly Chase pushed back from the faro table, stood up and faced Glen. He hooked his thumbs in his gunbelt and smiled. The piano player dropped his hands from the keyboard and the room went very quiet. Glen took another sip of whiskey. The look on Chase's face told him all he needed to know—there was trouble coming.

"Well, I'll be damned," Chase drawled. "Look what just crawled out of the barnyard!"

There were some low snickers and Glen's eyes traveled the length of the room. It was Chase Lawson's crowd and he was playing to his audience. Glen took a deep breath and expelled it slowly. He would get no help. It looked like he might have bitten off more than he could chew.

"Hello, Chase," he said. "I hear you're buying drinks for everyone these days. Thought I'd drop in and have one on Howard Trimmer myself."

Chase scowled. "The drinks I buy come out of my own pocket, Collins. Mr. Trimmer has nothing to do with it."

"Have it your way, Chase. But the fact is that Trimmer fills your pocket, so what's the difference?"

"Why don't you mosey back to the barn where you came from, boy. I can smell your horse manure from clear back here."

Glen finished his whiskey and placed it carefully on the table. "I'm empty, Chase. How about one on Trimmer?"

Lawson's face contorted with anger. "I told you! I'm doing the buying! Not Mr. Trimmer." He advanced and stopped in the middle of the room. His eyes dropped and he sneered. "You ain't even packing a gun."

"That's right," Glen said agreeably. "I just came over for a couple of free drinks on Trimmer."

"Damnit, quit saying that! I'm warning you, Collins."

It was working. Before Glen had even entered the Blue Beard he'd known this would be the sore spot in Chase. No man liked being called bought. A man owed his loyalty to his outfit and boss, but everyone had to pay their own way. Glen smiled. He had Lawson's number. Common sense told him he ought to ease back and push no farther. But so far, common sense hadn't worked at all. If it weren't for common sense he'd have married Maria. They'd have found a way. Now, with Roy Winslow in town he might lose her.

No, he was tired of trying to do the smart thing. Prodding Chase wasn't smart. It wasn't smart one bit. But he knew if there was any chance at all of winning the election, and Maria, it was going to have to come from facing the opposition and fighting back. Maybe not with guns because he wasn't a complete fool, but any other way would have to do. And right now, he wanted a fight. Win or lose it didn't matter. He'd been pushed around enough and it was time to serve notice that Glen Collins was a man who meant business. He aimed to win the election—and Maria. Chase Lawson and Roy Winslow were in for a battle.

"Why ain't you wearing a gun?" Chase demanded. He swiveled around to the onlookers. "This man is supposed to be running for sheriff, boys. But he's afraid to pack a six-shooter 'cause he might get shot. Is this the kind you want to elect to keep the peace in San Diego?"

There was a low murmur of voices and shaking of heads. Chase rotated back, his face triumphant. "See," he said. "You ain't fit to be a sheriff. What would you do if somebody called you out and told you to fill your hand or light out of town?"

"I'd be wearing a gun if I was sheriff."

A look of contempt curled Chase's lips. "You're worthless, Collins. You don't want to be sheriff, what you really want is to parade around town wearing a badge and hoping that Silvas girl is impressed long enough to bed down with you."

Glen launched himself from the bar and drove forward

knocking over tables in his rush to get to Chase Lawson. At that moment, he was a wild man. He didn't think that Chase might draw his gun and shoot. He didn't think at all.

Chase did draw, but at the last minute he flipped the gun around and his powerful arm slashed down through Glen's fists and pistol-whipped his forehead. Glen's knees went out from under him and he crashed to the floor. A terrible pain blossomed inside his head and he felt blood river down his face. Through the pain, he heard Chase laughing. Glen didn't move for almost a full minute. He just listened to them laughing and tried to concentrate on the gap between the floor planks. It was undulating like a sidewinder going up a sand dune. Glen squeezed his eyes shut and opened them again and again. He had to be able to focus! What a fool he was! He'd been thinking he was baiting Chase when all the time the man had waited until the right moment to speak the name that would make him blind with rage. He played me like a child, Glen thought.

"Come on boys, I'm buying drinks on the house!" Lawson called. "I guess there ain't much doubt about who is man enough to make a real sheriff."

Finally, the gap in the floor stopped squirming. Glen took a deep breath and stood up. He swayed forward and said thickly, "If it's your money and not Trimmer's I'll have a drink."

Chase smirked and laughed. "See folks, sometimes the only thing that can get through a skull-head is a little pistol-whipping." He motioned to the bartender.

"Give the boy a whiskey on me. Then I'm going to send him back to the barnyard where he belongs. Tonight we're drinking to San Diego's first sheriff—Chase Lawson!"

Glen leaned against the bar and avoided looking at anyone. He'd thought he was ready to come up when he left the floor but he was wrong. The moment he stood up, the room had begun to spin. He held onto the bar for support and took deep breaths. The blood from his scalp was back in his eyes. Glen reached up and touched the wound and grimaced. "Bring me a wet towel, bartender."

The bartender glanced over at Chase.

"Go ahead, let him have it," Chase ordered. "No, wait, give it to me. I'll scrub his face like I would a snot-nosed kid."

Glen knew he was out of time. Desperate, he grabbed a bottle of whiskey from the bar. He took a long pull and felt its fire burn the cloudiness from his mind. It was now or never.

"Here, turn around," Chase snarled, pulling him roughly by the shoulder.

Glen offered no resistance. He pivoted and waited until Chase lifted the towel, then he drove a right hand into Chase's gut with every ounce of strength he possessed.

Chase's mouth flew open like a beached fish. His eyes dilated and a great whoosh of air exploded from his lungs. He rocked forward, gasping for air. That's when Glen smashed him on the jaw. Chase careened backward across the room, knocking tables and chairs flying. He hit the far wall and sagged to his knees.

Glen reached down and picked up the wet towel. He wiped his own face clean then walked over and knelt above Lawson. He wrung the towel and Chase spluttered, thrashed, and coughed.

Glen returned to the bar and surveyed the hushed crowd.

"Now it's my turn," he said digging into his pockets. He yanked out Stewart's money and slammed it down hard. "I'm buying for the house and this is my own hard-earned money. There are no strings attached."

His eyes raked the crowd. "Any man says different, he answers to me!"

Three guns slid from leather. Glen swiveled slowly about to face them. He'd known it was coming—now it was up to them. "If you boys shoot," he said, "you'll hang. Every man here is a witness that I'm unarmed. Even Howard Trimmer can't change that."

The tallest one glanced at his friends. He glared around the room and seemed to be trying to make up his mind. At last, he growled to the men at his side. "Get Chase into a chair. I'll take care of our friend."

Glen waited while they dragged Lawson to his feet. They tried to lead him but suddenly he shook them free. "Let go of me!" he yelled. "Dave, put that gun away!"

The gun barrel slid from Glen's stomach and he felt a sigh escape his lips. Now it was up to Chase. They were both hurt; it was going to be an even fight.

Chase knotted his fists. "This is between you and me, boy. You caught me with a sneak punch and it damned sure won't happen again. I'm going to teach you a lesson you'll remember the rest of your life. I'm going to cripple you so you never forget. Now come and take it like a man."

Glen had no intention of waiting. He charged Lawson head on. They crashed together and grappled for a moment, fighting for the advantage. Glen felt a leg swing out behind him and realized Lawson was trying to trip him down, then start stomping. Lawson lowered his head and butted Glen in the face again and again. Glen smashed his boot heel down on the man's toe and broke free. He caught a punch in the chest and managed to sidestep a roundhouse swing that sent Lawson reeling off balance. Glen jumped in quickly and pounded twice to his opponent's ribs as Lawson swept by. For a moment, they both paused, gasping for air. "Goddamn you," Lawson panted, "stand still and fight!"

"I'm waiting," Glen rasped, "come on!"

Lawson charged with his head down. Glen tried to get in a blow but the man didn't give him a target. Before Glen could escape, Lawson had him in a bear hug and was squeezing his ribs until Glen was sure they'd crack. The man was incredibly strong! Somehow, Glen managed to get a forearm across Lawson's face. With his free hand he pounded Lawson's ear until the man roared with pain and broke his hold.

Glen swarmed in with his fists. They stood toe to toe and hammered at each other, neither asking or giving quarter. Chase was the harder puncher; he put his weight behind everything he threw. But Glen was faster and in better condition. The condition began to pay off and Glen could feel the power leaving Chase's arms. He pulled forward hitting harder and faster.

Chase reeled back and kicked. Glen twisted and caught the man's boot. He roared and threw the leg high into the air. Lawson slammed to the floor and Glen waited, his fists ready. Lawson pushed himself erect, but before he could raise his hands, Glen chopped him down.

"Get up," Glen rasped. "Get up! It's not over."

Lawson crawled to his hands and knees. He lifted his head. Hate and blood masked his face. "Get . . . get your gun," he choked. "If you don't get a gun I swear I'll come looking for you tonight!"

Glen lowered his fists, "I'll be back," he said between clenched teeth. "And I'll be packing iron." Then he wheeled around and stumbled for the door.

"Collins!"

Glen stopped and looked back toward the tall cowboy named Dave. "You do as Chase says, or we'll hunt you down like a dog."

Glen nodded woodenly and staggered through the swinging saloon doors.

Outside he collided with Juan Francisco Silvas. Juan was a small man, but strong. He grabbed Glen and held him erect. "Señor Glen," he whispered urgently, "you must hide! I was on my way home when I heard the fight. They will kill you!"

The night air was fresh and cool. Glen took several deep lungfuls and felt better. He glanced back at the saloon and then he began walking with Juan hurrying along at his side.

"Where are you going?" Juan asked.

"To get my gun. You heard what they said. If I don't return they'll come after me. I can't let that happen because if it did, they'd have to kill Hap too."

The old saddlemaker grabbed him by the arm. Glen stopped. "Juan, I have to go back to meet them. Don't you understand? They've given me no choice."

"If you do this, my friend, they will kill you," Juan said, shaking his head sadly. "It would not be a fair fight. You might outdraw Señor Lawson. But what of the others?"

"I don't know," Glen sighed. "Maybe they'll stay out of it."

Juan was a gentle man, never known to anger. But this time, Glen heard bitterness in his voice. "Don't be a fool! If you do not wish to think about yourself, think of Maria."

Glen bowed his head in despair. "I am, Juan. Always, I think about Maria. If . . . if anything should go wrong, I want Maria and Hap to have my livery. Tell Hap I said that. Do it for me, Juan, as a favor."

"Don't do this, Señor Glen! I beg of you. I have known for a long time about your love for Maria and I pray for the day when I can greet you as my son."

Glen studied the old man's face and felt a great affection for Juan Francisco Silvas. The man had spoken from his heart and Glen was grateful. "Thank you," he said, "for letting me know that. Now, I must go."

"Señor Glen . . ." Juan's voice cried.

Glen kept moving and inside, he felt very, very cold. He forced his mind away from Maria and her father. If he was to have any chance at all, he had to concentrate on drawing his gun and killing Chase Lawson. There was just no other way.

Maria Silvas heard the door slam and sat up, her attention immediately focused on Juan's face. Even before her father spoke she knew something was terribly wrong.

"Maria! Maria, we must do something quick or Señor Glen will be killed."

She was on her feet. "Father, what is wrong!"

It took less than a minute before she heard the story. By then, her eyes were wide with fear and her heart seemed to thunder inside. She had to think! She paced back and forth across their room for several minutes.

"Maria," her father was saying. "You must go stop him! Maybe he will listen to you."

She shook her head rapidly. "It would do nothing—only waste precious time. Those men would come after him, father. Glen knows that and he would not be hunted like an animal. I couldn't ask him to run."

"But he'll be shot. There are four men. He has no chance."

Maria grabbed her shawl and ran toward the door. "He must have help. I will find it for him!"

There was only one man she knew who might be able to save Glen, or at least see that he had a chance to live. And that man was Roy Winslow. Maria's feet flew down San Diego Avenue. But would Roy risk his own life to save a rival? He had to! Somehow she would appeal to him.

At last she was there. Maria, hair tangled and breathless, pounded on Josh Winslow's door. Then she grabbed the doorknob and burst inside.

Both Josh and Roy were half out of their chairs. Josh was in a smoking jacket, a cigar dangled from his lips as he looked at her with surprise. Roy hurried around his brother and grabbed Maria by the arm. "What's wrong?"

"It is Señor Glen Collins. He is going to the Blue Beard Saloon to meet Chase Lawson." She looked at the shocked expression on both men's faces. She had to make them understand. "Don't you see! This is what they want. He has no choice. If he doesn't go, they said they would hunt him down."

"How many, Maria?" It was Roy speaking. His voice was calm but urgent.

"Señor Lawson and three others!"

Roy whirled and raced down the hallway for his gun. Josh tore off his smoking jacket. "I'm going with you," he said. "Gunfighting is against the law. Both Chase and Glen know that. We will stop them."

Roy came running back. Maria saw him frantically buckling his gunbelt to his side. Then he bent over and tied the holster to his leg.

"Thank you!" she cried with relief. "I only hope we are not too late."

At that moment they heard gunfire. Maria grabbed the door. "It is too late," she whispered.

"The fool!" Roy swore. "Watch Maria," he yelled running for the street.

CHAPTER 5

When Glen left Juan Francisco he hurried to his Blackhawk Livery and climbed to the hayloft. It was totally dark but he knew the way by touch. He heard the gentle snoring of Hap Hazard and hesitated over the old man's bed. There were things he wanted to tell Hap. Mostly he wished to thank the old man for sticking it out through hard times and for being like the father he'd never known. But it was too late for that now. Hap would never let him face Lawson and the other three cowboys alone. Glen knew he'd have to tie Hap to his bed. The old man was a fighter; he'd grab his Sharps rifle and wind up getting killed.

Glen gazed out their window toward San Diego Bay and the thought struck him that only two people counted in his life—Maria and Hap. And now, when the odds said he was about to die, he couldn't tell either one of them about his feelings.

He angrily forced himself to think of other things. Things like how to survive the next half hour. Glen shrugged philosophically; there was always a chance unless a person gave up. Giving up wasn't in Glen. He dug his gun out and strapped it on. At the doorway he hesitated. "So long, pardner, I'll try and remember how to draw like you told me. I'll . . ." The words wouldn't come anymore and there was nobody listening anyway.

Outside, he walked to the horse trough and cupped water to his face. His gun hand was swollen and puffy from striking Lawson's face. Glen plunged it into the cold water and wiggled his fingers stiffly. Chase Lawson would have the same problem, Glen thought, touching a swollen cheekbone. Maybe they'd both be so stiff-handed they'd drop their guns trying to kill each other.

For some crazy reason he laughed out loud at the picture that formed in his mind so clearly. Two men vying for sheriff in a traditional gunfight. Suddenly, they go for their guns and—incredibly—both dropped them on the floor. The eager faces of the bloodthirsty onlookers gaped with astonishment, then disgust. At that point, both men would be hauled to jail for impersonation.

The picture faded and the smile disappeared. It wouldn't happen that way—someone was going to die. Glen pulled his hand from the cold water and dried it on his shirtfront. It was time.

When he rounded the Plaza, Glen saw the crowd waiting in the street. He drew up for a moment and his lips curled with anger. He saw people hurrying from side streets and their voices were loud and excited. Glen stood in the dark and felt his heart pounding. He lifted his gun and eased it back gently into his holster. Then he began walking.

As he came down the middle of the street someone yelled, "There he is!" The crowd became silent and parted as he strode toward the Blue Beard Saloon. Thank God, he thought, Maria is asleep and not here to see this.

Glen stepped up on the boardwalk and halted before the bat-wing saloon doors. He inspected the room and saw that they were waiting at the far end. One, two, three, four—all together with Chase in the middle. Glen put his hand on the door and slowly pushed it aside. He took two steps and came to wait.

"Keep coming, boy. We got the whole place to ourselves," Chase called.

"It seems," Glen said, "you've got a mite more company than me. I thought you'd be man enough to face this alone."

"They're out of it," Chase growled.

"Then why don't you ask them to drop their gunbelts to the floor?" Glen jerked a thumb toward the street. "Those folks outside aren't going to be real impressed with your courage, Chase. Not one damn bit, seeing as you had to be backed by three guns."

Chase scowled, he seemed to realize for the first time a crowd was outside.

"Don't listen to him, Chase!" the tall cowboy named Dave hissed. "He's a dead man doing a death rattle. Make your play."

"Yeah," Glen spat. "Go ahead. But just remember, if you live through this next five seconds you're going to be judged a coward. There's people watching through the windows, Chase. I imagine there will be quite a story in the *San Diego Union* Saturday."

Even across the room Glen could see the effect of his words. With his left hand, Chase wiped his lips nervously. "Go ahead, Dave," he said finally. "Do as he says. Drop your gunbelts."

Dave swore. "Don't be a fool! You're doing it his way. If you won't draw, let me. I'll kill him and you'll be out of it altogether."

Glen could feel the sweat popping up on his forehead. There wasn't much doubt that the tall man with the hatchet face and wild black hair was a gunfighter. He was the man with the speed and Glen resolved to take him out first if he managed to outdraw Chase Lawson.

"I said drop your belts," Chase repeated. "Mr. Trimmer wouldn't like reading that newspaper. I can take him easy."

Dave swore softly but he reluctantly followed directions. The other two men played follow the leader. Glen let out a deep breath and moved forward. "I'm a poor shot, boys, everyone knows that. I'd suggest you step away from Chase for your own good health."

They did, grudgingly. Not as far from their guns as Glen would have liked, but far enough. Suddenly, he felt a wild kind of joy as though he'd just gotten a reprieve from the gallows. Before, there had been no chance at all; now it was just the two of them during the first moment, and that meant hope.

At twenty feet he planted his feet. "Any time you're ready. I hope your gun hand ain't all swollen up."

"Draw!" Chase spat.

When Chase's mouth opened, Glen knew what was coming. His hand streaked for his six-gun and his thumb cocked back the hammer as he drew. Their guns bucked together and Glen felt a bullet smack his holster and spin him around in a full circle. Chase fired again and something crashed behind the bar. Glen dropped to his knees and fired twice more. Chase Lawson screamed and fell over backward.

In the next instant, Glen saw the three cowboys diving for their guns. He snapped off a shot and dove over the bar top with the roar of gunfire booming in his ears.

"Take cover!" Dave yelled.

Glen scrambled along the walkway behind the bar. Two bullets left and three men coming after him. No time to reload. He heard a chair scrape loudly and then the sound of boots running. Glen popped up and fired. His bullet caught one of the cowboys in full stride and the man collapsed in midair. Glen ducked and bottles exploded off the wall overhead. He crawled again and this time didn't stop until he ran out of bar. He was closed in solid. No way out except at the far end near the front door.

One bullet. He fumbled for his cartridge belt but there wasn't time. He heard them coming. No surprises. Dave was a gunfighter—he'd been counting too.

Suddenly, a man jumped out at the far end. Glen was waiting. It was a straight shot down the length of the bar. He fired and the cowboy wheeled around and cascaded through the front window into the street.

Empty gun. Time had run out.

The sound of laughter. Harsh, terrible laughter. Then quiet. "You lose, mister. Stand up or I'll shoot you on your knees. You've got three seconds to live."

Glen stood up. He saw two men! Dave, with his gun leveled and, just inside the doors, Roy Winslow. Roy wasn't wearing that big Mexican sombrero but Glen could have recognized him across a mile. It was the way he stood and right now he was standing with his feet apart and his fingers splayed over his gun.

"Mister!" Roy shouted.

Dave wheeled. He never knew who shot him. Glen saw Roy dip his shoulder and the gun was in his hand spitting lead, slamming Dave across the room, stitching holes in his shirtfront, driving him to the floor. It was over.

Glen's ears rang with gunfire and the room stank of gunsmoke. He saw Roy drop his gun into his holster and casually survey the destruction. At that moment, Glen couldn't help but feel an overpowering sense of admiration for Winslow. The man grinned and nodded happily. He looked like he'd just walked into church or a bingo party; he was nerveless.

Roy whistled softly. "I don't believe it, Glen. You do all this yourself?"

"Yep," Glen nodded. "I guess I did. All except for the last one. He was the best and he had me cold. I owe you my life. I won't forget this."

Roy brushed his words off with a wave of the hand. He eyed Glen with unconcealed amazement and admiration. "I just don't believe it!" he repeated.

"Neither do I." Glen laid his empty gun on the bar. "I think this calls for a drink—on me."

"In that case, I'll pour," Roy said coming to the bar. "One thing I have to ask, first."

Glen found a bottle and two glasses. "Go ahead and ask."

"Well, you did real good, Glen. But I don't understand why you just stood up at the end. That jasper was going to plug a big hole in you. Did you know that Maria came running to get me? Hell, I might have been out or asleep and then . . ."

"Maria? She found you?"

"Well sure," Roy chuckled. "I can see from the expression on your poor beaten face you didn't know that."

"No I didn't. I met her father, but that was all."

Roy poured two glasses full. "Getting back to the question, though. Why'd you just stand up?"

"I ran out of bullets. He knew it and didn't give me time to reload."

"Huh." Roy fished into his pocket and brought out a derringer. "Some men learn how to throw a knife for just that kind of emergency. I've found one of these to be handy at such times."

"I'll remember," Glen said.

"How many bullets you keep in the cylinder? Five or six?"

"Six."

"That's good. You'll hear some say you should keep the hammer on an empty chamber. That's so if you drop your gun it won't accidently fire. Don't you believe that nonsense. The odds of an accident like that aren't worth thinking about. Stay with six in the cylinder and keep a hideaway like this derringer."

"I'll do 'er," Glen said.

"Might save your life." He took a deep swallow. "Ahh, that's good. Well, I guess this pretty well sews up the election for you."

Glen didn't have time to answer. The saloon doors burst open and he saw Maria. For a moment, he thought she was going to come flying into his arms. She gave a cry of joy and started forward. She stopped and studied the body at her feet. He saw her expression change, her mouth tighten. She closed her eyes. Then she opened them and looked around the room missing nothing. Two more bodies and a lot of spilled blood.

"This," she whispered, "is what you're drinking to. Señor Winslow . . . Glen? Did it have to be this way?"

Glen walked over and stood before her. "Yes," he said. "There was no choice at all."

"I believe you, Glen. It's just that . . ." Suddenly she whirled and was gone.

Glen stood rooted. He felt a hand on his shoulder and turned to Josh Winslow. Josh shifted uncomfortably. "Glen," he said, "I'm afraid you and Roy are under arrest."

"Arrest? What for!" Glen demanded.

Roy laughed. "Come on, Josh! You must be crazy. Hell, there's a whole street full of people out there who saw what happened. Glen ought to get a medal for this."

"A medal?" Josh's mouth twisted. "Four dead men and you're talking about medals! We have laws in San Diego to prevent this kind of . . . slaughter."

"There wasn't any choice," Glen said stubbornly. "Can't you understand? They were coming after me."

"Yeah," Roy snapped, "what would you have done if it was you they'd been after? Would you have put your tail between your legs and run?"

Josh sighed with resignation. "Probably not. I'd have met them and been carried out boots first. But don't you see," he argued, "that's all wrong! That's what we have laws for. To protect people's lives and to settle this kind of trouble without bloodshed."

Roy's voice filled with contempt. "Laws or no laws, there'll always be shootings. A man forces you to the wall, you have to fight back."

"And what," Josh said evenly, "forced you to come running down here? Damnit, Roy, you haven't changed at all. Any scent of trouble and you're charging in with both feet."

"He saved my life, Josh!" Glen shouted.

"Oh hell," Josh muttered. "I need a drink."

The three men stood at the bar in strained silence. A few of the townspeople started to come in and Josh yelled, "Get out of here. This saloon is closed."

Glen studied his drink a moment. "Josh, this was my fight and I'll go to jail if I have to. But Roy shot in self-defense. There's no justice in him going behind bars for what he did."

Josh leaned forward and spoke as if to himself. "Let's level. Just between the three of us. O.K.?"

They nodded.

"You have to understand my position as mayor. Glen, you're running for sheriff, and right now, it's a one-horse race. But that don't change things. If you go to jail and face the circuit judge, all this will come out in the open and you'll be cleared. Not only that, but the folks in this town will see that justice has been done. You'll win the election even if Trimmer suddenly comes up with another gunnie."

"You think he might?" Glen asked.

"Probably not. But if this thing doesn't go to court and get dismissed, you can bet he'll raise a stink. He could say anything. Might even claim that you had friends upstairs that opened fire and then slipped away."

"That's crazy!"

"Sure it is," Josh argued. "But some people will believe anything. No offense, but you'd have to admit it's pretty hard to believe you killed Chase Lawson and two others all by yourself."

"Chase wasn't that fast. Maybe his hands were stiff and it could be he was still groggy from being hit in the fight. I don't know or care. I just feel lucky."

"You should. And like it or not you've built a reputation in one night. But the point is," Josh continued, "Judge Bonner comes through in just five days and we need this thing done up legal and out in the open. You can't afford to become sheriff with anyone thinking there was a cover-up."

"I understand," Glen said finally. "But what about Roy? Why should he go to jail?"

"Same reasons," Josh said quickly. He shook his head. "No, that's not true. Roy, I admire what you did for Glen. But the fact is you weren't forced to defend yourself like he was. You could have stayed out of it."

A look of disbelief overcame Roy's face. "Are you serious! I couldn't let a man get shot down in cold blood. You didn't see what I did, Josh. That tall fella was taking a head on Glen and he was out of bullets. He was going to execute him!"

"That's the truth," Glen said.

"Then we'll tell it in court and you'll both be heroes!" Josh slammed his fist on the bar. "Don't you see that Roy has to go to court if he's got a chance of making this his home? If he doesn't, folks will just say he got off because his brother is mayor."

"Seems to me," Roy said tightly, "that's what it all boils down to—your reputation."

Josh whirled on his brother. "Don't say that again, Roy. You've been in trouble all your life and I'm not going to let you botch this up in my town. You're going to stand trial before Judge Bonner and I guarantee you'll walk out with a clean slate and no one will be able to say I pulled strings. Do you understand me?"

Roy poured another drink and Glen saw his hand shook; he wasn't nerveless after all. He splashed the whiskey down fast and poured another. "I didn't tell you, Josh," he said hoarsely. "I was thrown in jail down in Sonora, Mexico. They kept me for almost nine months."

"What . . . what for?" Josh said placing his glass down quickly.

"Oh, you know." Roy tried a laugh that died on his lips. "Same old thing. Killed a man over a young señorita. He was jealous and drunk. Then I had to shoot his brother. It was . . . was a fair fight."

"Sure!" Josh spat. "They were mad and probably both drunk. And you, being lightning fast with a six-shooter just did what had to be done. Is that right?"

"Cut it out, Josh!" Roy shouted, pushing back from the bar. "You may be my big brother but you ain't my judge and jury. I didn't want to kill them brothers any more than I wanted to drill this man tonight. I even gave him a warning before I drew my gun. It was his choice to die! Not mine. I pulled iron in self-defense."

"That's true, Josh. His name was Dave and he was a gunman himself."

"I see," Josh scowled. "I apologize, Roy."

"Aw, forget it. But, Josh, I purely don't want to go behind bars again—even for five days." He seemed to shiver. "Down in Mexico their jails would make your skin crawl. There wasn't much light and the air was so stinking and hot I was always sick."

"We have a new jail," Josh said quickly. "We been needing one for a long time and especially now that we're going to have a sheriff. There's plenty of light, Roy. And it's clean. It wouldn't be anything like the one in Mexico."

"I don't care!" Roy's eyes were wild. "I can't stand being caged. The walls seem to come in on me."

"I kind of feel that way, myself," Glen said.

"You do?"

"For a fact," Glen tried to make it sound convincing. "I can't hardly go inside a cave, without the jitters. I don't know what it is but a small space seems to grow smaller on a man. If I think about it, even my chest seems to tighten."

"That's how I feel!" Roy exclaimed. There was a flood of relief on his face. He laughed. "We ought to make some pair. Both of us going crazy together."

"I guess we will," Glen smiled. He reached over behind the bar and grabbed two full bottles of whiskey. "Any law on the books yet about drinking in the jug?"

"Not to my knowledge," Josh said.

"Then let's get out of here before me and Roy change our minds."

Outside, the crowd opened and the three men paraded down San Diego Avenue to the new jail. Josh pulled a set of keys out of his vest pocket and fumbled in the darkness until he found the right one. He opened the door and reached up for a lantern beside the doorway. "Got a match?"

Glen struck one with his thumbnail and the light flickered and grew strong. The jail held no surprises for him. He'd visited it several times and already had a place picked where he'd put a desk. The building was made out of adobe. The walls were three feet thick all the way around. In the front half, the room was bare and would be used as the sheriff's office. Across the rear stood the bars and two cells. Those bars were strong and set deep. Glen knew because he'd placed them himself. Each cell had a chamber pot, bunk with a straw mattress, and a pail for holding water. Neither bed had pillows, but two new blankets lay folded on each.

Roy's eyes were riveted on the bars.

Glen forced a laugh. "Almost nicer than a hotel. This ain't going to be bad at all."

Roy took a deep breath. "Sure." He unbuckled his gun and handed it over to Josh. "If you weren't my brother, I'd never do this."

"I know, Roy. Thanks. When you get out we'll start talking about your future. I've got enough money to set you up in business. Just a loan to get you rolling. You'll see things are going to start going your way here. And I'm proud of what you did tonight."

Glen looked away quickly. Josh's eyes were misty and Glen could see their mayor was doing something that hurt. But he was doing what was right and both Roy and he understood. He guessed Josh Winslow had probably been born a wise man.

Glen unbuckled the gunbelt and passed it over to Josh. "You two can stand here jawing all night but I intend to stretch out on that bunk and have a drink."

He opened the cell door and stepped inside. For a moment, he felt an overpowering urge to back out. But he forced himself to reach back and pull the door shut with a click. There. He was locked in. Maybe there was one good thing about all this—he'd know how it felt to be a prisoner. Glen sat down on the bunk and forced gaiety into his voice. "Yes, sir," he called to the brothers. "A five-day vacation is what I'm planning to take. Josh, I hope you plan on seeing we get something besides beans to eat."

"You'll probably have half the town in here visiting before the week's out. I'd be willing to bet the ladies will be sending food over by the platter. Watch out or you'll get fat."

"Afraid there isn't enough time," Glen said ruefully. "Don't suppose you could wire Judge Bonner and have him delay his arrival a week or two."

"Cut it out!" Roy yelled at both of them. Then, just as quickly he marched into the cell and slammed the door locked behind. For a moment, he stood like he was frozen. Then Glen saw him relax and when he revolved back toward the office his face was composed.

"I'm sorry," he said. "It's just that I knew you were saying all that to make me feel better. Thanks but you can cut the act. This is a jail and we're locked up like animals. But I can take it for five days. I'm going to be all right."

Josh looked between the bars at his brother. "Of course you are. I'll be in and out checking on you both during the day. And you'll have lots of company."

"None for me," Roy said. "I don't know a soul in San Diego. No time to meet any women except . . . except Maria."

Glen took a drink. "She'll be by, Roy. I'm willing to bet on it."

"Good. It's amazing how a beautiful woman can lift my spirits." He glanced up at Josh. "You better get home. Donna will be worried sick. Tell her I appreciate fixing up a room for me but won't be able to use it for a while. Tell her to keep it ready because I'll be back."

"Sure," Josh said. "Good night my friends."

They drank quietly for what Glen figured to be almost an hour. He sipped very slowly for he wasn't a hard-drinking man. At first, Roy paced back and forth across his cell. He held the bottle by the neck and every two or three trips back and forth he'd throw it up to his lips and take a deep pull. Glen noticed that, after the first few minutes, Roy didn't even seem to look at anything. He took a measured number of steps until Glen thought sure he was going to walk straight upright into the wall. Then, at the last second, he'd do an about-face and stride back across the room. Josh had turned down the lamp but there was still enough light for Glen to see that the man's handsome young face was like a steel mask. Expressionless and unseeing. What was going on inside Roy's head?

Finally, Glen stood up and sauntered over to the bars that separated them. "What's the matter?" he asked gently.

Roy halted and seemed to shake himself out of a fog. "Do you really want to know?"

"Wouldn't ask if I didn't."

"No, I guess not. You don't strike me as a man who prattles for nothing. O.K.," he sighed. "I'll tell you. It's Maria."

"What about her?" Glen said, holding his breath.

"Well, you saw me walk her home. We talked a long time."

"About what?" Glen tried to keep his voice under control. There was nothing wrong with talking.

"Oh, nothing really important. I told her about what women wore in the places I've been."

"Yeah," Glen said roughly. "I bet you're a real expert on that."

"Damnit," Roy blurted. "You asked and I told you the

truth. You should have seen her face! She got all interested and excited. Said she'd like to hear more."

"She's interested because she probably wants to do a story for the newspaper." It was a mean, cutting thing to say and Glen saw Roy deflate with disappointment. He relented and was sorry. "Ah, she probably was interested for herself, too," he added lamely.

"I . . . I know she was. She's really special, isn't she."

"Yeah, she's special all right. I plan to marry her before long."

"But you never asked her."

"How do you know that?"

"Because I asked her if you did. That means she's free to see whoever she wants."

Glen waited a long moment before he spoke. "Tell me something, Roy; would it make any difference if we were engaged?"

Roy took a drink. His eyes narrowed. "Not a damn bit."

"That's what I thought. I also figure the only reason you came along and saved my life is because Maria begged you."

"That's true. I'm not as big a fool as Josh thinks. I want to stay alive. But one thing you should know."

"What's that?" Glen asked.

"If I'd have been there, on my own, I'd have done the same for any man. I'm not a killer and I can face myself in the mirror every morning with a clear conscience. I wouldn't have let that man cold-bloodedly murder you—Maria or no Maria."

The anger washed out of Glen. "You did save my life—reason be damned. And now that you've seen Maria you're going after her."

Roy nodded his head solemnly.

"So be it," Glen sighed. He lifted the bottle. Maybe he would get drunk after all. "May the best man win."

Roy returned the salute. "To the better man." Then he resumed his animal-like pacing far into the night.

CHAPTER 6

Glen awoke with the sun's rays filtering through the jail bars. He opened his eyes and started, then relaxed. There was nothing to get up for, nothing to do. He peered over at Roy. The man was asleep and probably would be for another hour.

Roy's pacing had finally stopped in the dark, early morning hours. Glen listened to the growing sounds of the town coming alive for another day of business. He heard a wagon roll by on the street and a rooster crow. Hap Hazard would be stirring and the old man would come hunting him before the hour was past.

Glen tried to go back to sleep. The light grew strong and he heard children laughing on their way to school. Sleep was impossible. All his life he'd risen at daybreak and worked past sundown. He liked to keep busy and moving. It was his firm belief that active people were better off all the way around. They didn't get fat; they were happier too. Nothing brought a body down faster than having too much time to think. Too much thinking was bound to lead to worry. Five days in jail, he thought, pinned up next to a man who paces all night and wants to steal my girl. Yeah, he had plenty to worry about.

Glen pushed himself off the bunk and stretched his long muscles. He sauntered over to the jail bars and gazed out his small window. To the northeast, he could see the crumbled remains of the old presidio. Many years earlier, it had housed the Spanish, then later Mexican, garrisons. But with the Treaty of Guadalupe Hidalgo, California had been ceded by Mexico to the United States. The presidio itself was now in ruin. Even the Mission San Diego de Alcalá, six miles inland, was decaying. There wasn't much left—a few Catholic priests struggled to cultivate the land and save the souls of local Indians. Even now, as Glen watched, he saw a mission Indian lead a horse-drawn *carreta*. The mission was the only place that still used those great wooden-wheeled carts. He guessed they couldn't afford much better. The Indian passed by on his way down to the harbor to try to sell his produce. Most likely the sacks contained nuts and dried fruit.

Behind him, Glen heard the jail door open and he turned to see Hap Hazard and Maria Silvas.

He smiled and touched his lips with a forefinger, motioning to the sleeping Roy Winslow. He met them at the bars.

Hap spoke first. "If you weren't already in trouble," he growled, "I'd try and whip you! I'm madder than a wet cat."

Glen smiled, his eyes flicked to Maria. She was standing back, her face expressionless. He returned his attention to Hap. "It worked out fine. I guess the shooting practice saved my life."

"You should have woke me up and asked for help!"

"Shhh," Glen hissed. "He's asleep."

Hap glared over at Roy. "I don't give a hoot if he wakes up or not."

"Well, I do. I owe the man my life."

Hap stiffened. "I didn't hear about that part. What'd he do it for?"

Again, Glen's eyes met Maria's. "He did it for you, Maria. But that don't matter. Hap, you said I should have asked for help. Well, you're right."

"You admit it, then?" Hap looked surprised.

"Yes I do. So I'm going to ask right now. Can you take care of things until I'm free? It should only be five days."

Hap nodded. "Sure," he grunted. He twisted around and pulled Maria forward. "Here. She's the one you need to talk with. Me, I got a heap of work to do so I'll mosey. Be back later."

"So long, Hap," Glen said.

When the door closed Maria moved up to the bars and grasped them tightly. "Glen," she whispered, "are you all right?"

"Yes."

"I am sorry I ran last night. I haven't been able to sleep thinking about the way I acted."

He covered her hands with his own. "Don't worry. It was a pretty rough sight you walked into. I can imagine your shock."

She rested her forehead on the bars. "I was so afraid for you. I felt certain you were dead. And when I saw you standing there . . . I couldn't believe my happiness. But when I looked around and saw all those bodies, all the happiness was gone. So many men."

He lifted her chin and kissed her between the bars. Her lips were soft and met his own eagerly.

Glen smiled. "If these bars weren't holding me back, you'd be in trouble, señorita."

"I might wish it were so," she blushed. "Glen?"

"Yes."

"Are you going to ask me to Señora Estudillo's fiesta?"

He groaned. "I completely forgot about it!"

"Does it mean so little to you?"

"Of course not, Maria. Will you accompany me?"

She nodded happily. "I only heard about it yesterday. Señora came by the newspaper office to ask me what I would wear. She was very angry at you for not asking me."

"I am a fool."

"Sometimes," Maria teased. Then her face grew serious. "Glen, Señora Estudillo wants me to wear a dress she wore long ago. She spoke of dancing with Jose Antonio in this dress. I think it would bring her joy."

"Then you should," Glen said.

"I think so, yes."

"Good! It is settled." Her face flushed with excitement. "We will make a handsome couple dancing together."

"Sure we will," Glen lied. What was he going to do now? He didn't even know how to dance. He decided to face that later. Right now there was too much happiness in her face to tell her the truth.

She handed him a folded napkin and he felt its warmth.

"I baked some bread for you and Señor Roy. Now, I must go to work. Señor Ames will be anxious to print the story of last night. I will have to talk to many people this morning. But already I know what they will say."

"Tell me."

"All right. They will say you are a brave man who deserves to be sheriff. They will say the town will be safe with Sheriff Glen Collins on duty."

"I hope so. I will do my best. Maria," he said, "come closer."

She did and he reached through the bars and kissed her again. Breathless, she finally pulled free.

"It is a good thing indeed that you are behind bars!" She laughed softly. "You are a changed man."

"I'm alive to see this new day and I feel good being able to touch and kiss you." He thought for a moment.

This was a perfect time to be poetic. Think man! "Your lips, Maria . . ."

"Yes," she said eagerly.

"Your lips are as soft and full as . . . as a horse's coat in wintertime."

Laughter exploded from Roy Winslow. Maria glared over at Roy and his laughter rattled to silence. She looked back at Glen. "That was," she said, choosing her words carefully, "a very . . . very nice thing to say. Good-by, Glen."

When she'd gone, Roy squealed, "Horse's coat in wintertime? I don't believe it!"

"Shut up!" Glen said angrily. His face burned with humiliation. "Stop laughing or I swear I'll tear you in half."

Roy finally seemed to catch his breath. He wiped tears from his face. "Yee God, are you ever a smooth-talking Don Juan."

"It wasn't that bad," Glen said hotly.

"Oh no. Not bad at all," Roy smirked. "Keep it up and I haven't a thing to worry about. Maria will come running into my arms."

"You keep poking fun at me and you won't have any arms!"

Roy sat up. "Remember, I saved your life."

"I can be forgetful."

"Yeah," Roy said, "and the first thing you better forget is trying to charm a woman with words. 'Cause you ain't got it. *Comprehende?*"

"All right, if you're so good, what would you have said."

"Not a damned thing. After I kiss a señorita the last thing they want me to do is to start talking."

Glen knotted his fists. "Well, the kind you're used to kissing isn't like Maria."

"You know something? I think you may be right—up to

a point. With her I'll have to go a little slower." He grinned wolfishly. "But the end result will be the same."

"The hell it will! You step out of line and I'll break you."

Roy yawned with disdain. "I'm getting a little weary of your threats, blacksmith. Besides, you don't own Maria. She's free as a bird and I reckon she's ready to fly. I aim to teach her."

Glen bottled up his rage and stared out the window. The day had gone sour.

"I'm mighty curious," Roy said. "Curious enough to make a little bet."

"Bet on what?"

"I bet you dance like a loon. All feet and no grace."

"You lose," Glen said wearily. "I can't dance at all."

Roy chuckled. "Figures. I should have guessed as much. What are you going to do come fandango time?"

"You have big ears."

"What was I supposed to do? Cover them? Man, come the big party and you're going to go from hero to clown. That's where I step in."

"You haven't even been invited," Glen muttered.

"That's no problem. In a town this small that Señora Estudillo is bound to invite the mayor. She and my brother are friends, right?"

Glen didn't answer. Everyone, including the Señora, liked their *alcalde*, mayor.

"So how is she going to invite him without me? I know the Spanish customs better than you do and that would be an insult." Roy waited for an answer. When none came, he demanded. "Well, isn't that true?"

"Yeah," Glen finally admitted.

"Well then I'll see you there. You'll have two choices and I'm going to enjoy either one. Dance and make a fool out of yourself or sit it out and let me take over." He stood up. "You wait until they see me dance *el jarabe*. Goes like this."

Glen saw him place his hands behind his back and began to dance striking his boot heels on the floor to a rhythm, spinning in quick circles. After several minutes Roy stopped and laughed. "Go ahead, Glen, give it a try. It's simple!"

"I'll tell you what's simple, Winslow. You and me are going to lock horns."

"I've seen you shoot and I'm not going to lose any sleep worrying. And you've seen me in action and that ought to be enough, even for a simple man, to make you go easy with your threats."

"I can back up my words."

Roy scoffed. "Don't make a fatal mistake. I'm not Chase Lawson and your luck only stretches so far. I wouldn't want to be the one who plants you, Glen—Maria wouldn't like that one bit. But if you force me, I'll have no choice. And as for Maria, she'd get over it in time. I'd be good medicine for her broken heart."

"You'd poison her!" Glen spat. "I'd kill you before that."

"No you wouldn't, you'd be dead. Remember?"

Glen slumped down on his bed and stared at the ceiling. He wasn't going to make any more threats. He didn't have any way to back them up. It was going to be a long five days.

During the rest of the day, Glen began to realize that he'd become a celebrity. The most prominent men in San Diego all found time to visit the jail and wish him their best. Even A. E. Horton, the wealthy promoter of the budding settlement called "New Town" San Diego, came.

On Saturday, when the *San Diego Union* paper was distributed, the steady trickle of visitors became a torrent. Strangers, wives, and even children dropped by to see him. The kids were a particular delight to Glen, some stood by the door and stared at him with round and wonderous eyes. A few were brave enough to ask for autographs. Glen signed but felt foolish. He wasn't made to feel any easier by Roy Winslow.

For some strange reason, most people seemed to dismiss Roy's part in the Blue Beard Saloon. It was Glen Collins, their home-town boy, who'd killed three men in self-defense. Again and again Glen tried to play up Roy's importance but the townspeople stubbornly refused to listen.

One night, when they were alone, Glen questioned him about it. "You seem," he began, "mighty quiet."

Roy was lying on his back smoking a cigar. He puffed thoughtfully. "You've been talking enough for both of us."

"I've been trying to explain to everyone how you came and saved my life."

"Yeah, I know you have. But they don't hear you and that's fine with me. I'm not running for office and I don't wany any pats on the back for what I done. All I want is out of this cage."

"Well," Glen said, "the day after tomorrow Judge Bonner arrives."

"The fiesta is just a few days later, isn't it?"

"That's right," Glen answered.

"Have you figured out what you're going to do come dance time?"

"I'll just have to tell Maria the truth."

Roy snorted with disgust. "Hell, that's no way. You know, I feel sort of bad about this Maria thing. If I wasn't so taken with her, I'd let you have her all to yourself."

"That's mighty big of you," Glen replied sarcastically.

Roy seemed to have missed the heavy sarcasm in Glen's voice. "You're not a bad sort," he continued. "And you're sure as hell going to be no competition. Look at the way you dress! Like a carpetbagger. Can't dance and everytime you try and say something romantic you make me laugh." He shook his head sadly. "You're no competition at all. Kind of takes the pleasure out of it. Like kickin' a kid around."

"Spare me the pity," Glen snapped angrily. Who the devil did Roy think he was?

"I'll tell you what," Roy said bouncing to his feet. "I feel bad about this and my conscience is bothering me. I'm going to give you a break. The chance of a lifetime. I'm going to teach you the basics."

"Of what?" Glen asked skeptically.

"Of everything! We'll get Josh to give us our guns back, empty of course, and smooth out your fast draw. You're doing better but I can show you how to shave off some time. But besides that, I'll teach you how to dress and act around a woman!" Roy's eyes danced with growing excitement.

"Yeah," he said, his voice rising with conviction. "It might even be fun! I never taught anyone my secrets but then I never seen anyone like you before. In the daytime we'll practice on your draw, at night, how to dance. What about it?"

Glen felt a surge of excitement and hope. But then, almost as quickly, suspicion. "Why would you want to do that? We're both after the same girl. Excuse me for doubting your motives, but I do."

"Of course you would! But that's only because you don't see yourself through my eyes. Oh," he laughed, "I'm not worried about Maria. No contest. Besides, I can't work miracles."

Glen pulled out his pocketknife and began cleaning his nails. He needed a moment to think it over. Was Roy that confident? He glanced up at the expectant and amused face. He sure appeared to be. What the heck, Glen thought, it might help pass the time and I've got nothing to lose. "All right," he said, "why not?"

"Good! You've got more sense than I thought. Now," he rushed, "the first thing tomorrow we send for the barber and you get a haircut. Not short, I'll tell him how. I'll ask Josh to give us back our guns so we can get started. In the meantime, we send for a tailor and order you some new clothes."

"Wait a minute!" Glen exclaimed. "That costs money."

"Sure it does. Are you broke or something?"

"Well, no. But I sure don't have a fat bank account."

Roy slumped down on his bunk. "Aw the hell with it," he said disgustedly. "I'm offering you something money can't buy—my experience. And all you can think of is a lousy seventy or eighty dollars."

"That much!" Glen choked.

"We'll do it right or not at all. New clothes top to bottom."

"What about my boots," Glen said pointing. "I could polish them up and . . ."

"They're clodhoppers! Run down at the heels. Toes all mashed in. I'm going to teach you how to dance, remember? You can't be out there dancing with Maria and tromping all over her like a plow horse." Roy shook his head gravely. "Nope, it's new boots or the whole deal's off."

Glen rubbed the back of his neck and paced his cell. It was a lot of money. For seventy or eighty dollars he could build new stalls or even whitewash the entire livery barn. He'd been wanting to do that for years.

Roy seemed to peer right into his thoughts. "You're thinking maybe you ought to spend that money fixing up your barnyard. I can tell by the look on your face. Well, go ahead. You probably never spent a dime on yourself in your entire life and never will. But I'll tell you something, friend."

"What's that?"

"If you go dressed to the señora's fiesta looking like I think you'll look, you'll insult both her and Maria. Remember what Maria said? She's going to wear the old lady's dress and you and her are supposed to remind Señora Estudillo of her wedding night. Maria can pull it off and put a shine in that old woman's eyes. But not you. Because you're too cheap to spend a few dollars you're going to look like a peon!"

"All right, damnit! You win. Tomorrow you help me practice the draw and I'll get a haircut and new clothes. I'll sell a horse or something."

Roy smiled with triumph. "That's the spirit!" He studied Glen's face for several minutes. "Well, there isn't much we can do about that," he said finally.

"About what?"

"Your face," Roy said. "Do you have to shave every day?"

"Of course, but . . ."

"That's good. Grow a mustache. The women love 'em. Shape it like I do. You don't want the thing looking like a strip of shriveled jerky, so taper it off with a flair."

"There isn't time," Glen protested.

"Sure there is. If it isn't grown in by the fiesta, then take a piece of charcoal from your forge and fill in."

"What about the dance?" Glen asked. He was starting to feel poorly about his appearance. He'd never considered himself handsome but neither did women and children lunge for cover when he passed.

"The dance? Oh yes. First, do you know how to ask for one?"

"Sure," Glen said. "All a fella has to do is to walk right up and say, 'Would ya like to dance with me?'"

"That's a great line," Roy chuckled, shaking his head with wonder. "Very original, too."

"All right, then! What do you say?"

"First you bow. Like this," Roy said, sweeping off his imaginary sombrero and bending at the waist. "Then you say something like, 'It would be a great honor to share this beautiful music with such an enchantment as yourself.' Now, you try it."

Glen did. He bowed deeply, repeated the invitation and straightened. Pretty good, he thought. "Well, how was I?"

"Not bad. Only you bowed so low that you asked her knees to dance. You don't have to bend that much. Just a little but with great respect. Now try it again. And this time slow it down. Let the words roll from your lips. The bow should be slow; you are not a puppet."

Glen, feeling like an idiot, bowed and carefully repeated the invitation. When he finished, Roy was smiling.

"Much better!" Roy said. "Now the hard part; the dancing itself. Do you know anything?"

"I've watched people before," Glen said hesitantly. "But I never tried."

"Well you will tonight. I'll show and teach you the waltz and the most beautiful and graceful dance of all—the *contradanza*."

"The what?" Glen asked.

"*Contradanza*. The waltz, of course, is just between a man and woman. But the *contradanza* involves others. They move together in an intricate series of steps and combinations borrowed from many dances. It embraces the most graceful movements of them all."

"Sounds a little complicated to me."

"It's worth the learning. Because it takes all the best of the other dances. It is poetry. Now, let us begin. Ahh," he sighed, "if only we had music."

Glen pulled his harmonica out from a bag of things Hap had brought earlier. "I could play a few tunes with this."

"Excellent! Play a waltz first and watch me, then follow exactly. For the *contradanza* you will have to play something much faster. And I will clap."

Glen started to play and Roy solemnly went through the waltz steps. Thank God, Glen thought, nobody is around to see this. He didn't quite believe it himself. But if this was what it took to avoid disappointing Señora Estudillo and Maria, then he'd do it. Roy didn't know it yet, but he was making a big mistake. Glen started to play and his eyes missed nothing as Roy slowly waltzed around the cell. I'm going to learn everything the man can teach me before I get out of here, he thought. And I'm going to work every spare minute of the day with a gun. There wasn't much time left; he was going to make the most of it.

Judge Bonner scowled out at the packed crowd. It was standing room only in the big Town Hall Building and the judge seemed nervous.

Glen shifted in his seat, glanced quickly at Maria and Roy, then looked back at the judge. Bonner was a short man, but still made a pretty imposing figure on the bench. The judge's face was round and red. He always looked as if he were out of breath and angry. He had a wild head of gray hair and a beard to match. The judge wore a set of wire-rimmed spectacles and had a habit of taking them off and putting them on every couple minutes. Right now the judge was putting them on again. He stood up and cleared his throat loudly.

"This court is in session. Now everybody please shut up!"

Roy nudged him and whispered. "Don't seem too friendly, does he?"

"He's hanged a few," Glen replied softly. "Don't get cute or try to stage a show for the ladies or . . ."

"Are you two deaf!"

Glen jerked erect. "No, sir!"

"No, sir," Roy echoed.

"O.K., then," Bonner said after a long piercing inspection that made Glen wither. "Let's get this sideshow over."

He pulled off his glasses and cleared his voice again. "Now you, Glen Collins, are accused of shooting three men dead five nights ago in the Blue Beard Saloon. That right?"

"Yes, your honor."

"Hmph. Hard to believe. And you, Roy Winslow, are accused of shooting a fourth. True?"

"Yes, your honor."

"Well, that simplifies things considerably." He glanced over at the court clerk. "Duly note the accused admit they plugged the four dead men."

The judge leaned forward. "Now, Glen Collins, I'll start with you. But first, I want to remind you that the laws of San Diego are clear and posted in the court clerk's office as well as in the post office. No shooting another person in town! I've been told you're running for sheriff, and in fact, one of the men you shot was your opponent. That right?"

Glen nodded woodenly. "Yes, your honor, but it was self-defense."

"Just answer my questions, young man. Gunning down your opponent is one of the oldest and most despicable ways of winning an election I can think of."

There was a low wave of laughter at the back of the room. Someone was heard to say, "And most effective."

"Silence!" the judge roared. He crammed his glasses over his ears. "Who said that? Who said it, I say!"

No one moved. The judge whirled around. "Clerk. Did you see who said that?"

"No, your honor," the man stammered.

"No guts," Bonner mumbled. "Now, Mr. Collins, you did break the law and I find it very difficult to see how you consider yourself fit to be elected sheriff having done so."

"Your honor?"

The judge scanned his crowd of onlookers. "It's a pity that your first sheriff is going to win by default. And that doesn't mean that I think he's unworthy of the office. But in this day and time, a sheriff has to be the best man a town can offer. We've all read and heard about the bad ones—killers and crooks shaking down people for protection or worse. Did you know that in the last ten years our country has hung six of its own sheriffs?"

Glen and Roy exchanged glances. Roy's face was alive with interest.

"I've sent some to prison myself. Because as far as I'm concerned, there is nothing more loathsome than a dishonest sheriff. And the man that becomes San Diego's first will be writing a page of California history. He'll either set the example as one where families are safe, or let the town degenerate into lawlessness. That is his charge. I find it a great disappointment that there aren't ten good men standing in line here wanting this office."

The judge's eyes bored into Glen. "And that is why I asked, How can you expect others to respect and follow the laws of San Diego when you, Glen Collins, did not?"

"Sir," Glen said. "I never broke one before and this won't happen again."

Judge Bonner almost smiled, but managed to cover it

up. "Of course it won't," he boomed. "There was only one other candidate for office and you got rid of him!"

Out of the corner of his eye, Glen saw Roy begin to shake with suppressed laughter. Roy was crazy. Glen felt sweat pour down his back. Josh had told them the judge would let them go with just a warning. He was beginning to wonder.

"Mr. Winslow! What the devil are you doing? Because if you're laughing, I'll send you right back to jail and you shall cackle away until the walls crumble."

"No, sir! I mean, your honor. I wasn't laughing."

Glen peered sideways. Roy seemed to finally get the message; he looked scared. His face was rigor mortis stiff.

"Mr. Winslow, I understand you are the younger brother of San Diego's mayor, Josh Winslow. That right?"

"Yes, sir."

"And I'm also told you were in town less than a day when you shot and killed a Mr. Dave Rady that night. True?"

"Yes, your honor."

"You work fast." The judge's eyes narrowed behind the bifocals. "You ever been in serious trouble before, young man?"

Glen heard Roy swallow drily, saw him glance over at his brother for help.

"Your honor," Josh said, coming to his feet. "This whole matter is very clear and has been witnessed by a half dozen of those present. It was a case of self-defense."

"In all due respect, Mayor, sit down and keep quiet." Josh sat and the judge again focused his attention to Roy. "Now, why don't you tell the court exactly what happened."

Roy took a deep breath and started talking. Glen listened as he told it from beginning to end. The room was very quiet when he'd finished and sat down.

The judge inspected his glasses. "Do you mean to tell me you walked in there with your gun holstered?"

"Yes, sir."

"At that moment you saw this Dave Rady taking aim on Glen Collins. Then you shouted a warning even before drawing your own weapon?"

"That's right, your honor. I thought if he saw I hadn't filled my hand he might surrender."

The judge shook his head in disbelief. "You took quite a chance, young man. You must have a great deal of confidence in yourself."

Roy shrugged. "I know my abilities," he said loud enough for everyone to hear.

"I'll bet you do," the judge said quietly. He gazed around the hall. "I heard about this shooting clear up in Los Angeles. I've read the *San Diego Union* and respect that paper for its honesty and ability to relate the facts without prejudice."

He rose from his seat. "As your respected mayor stated, this appears to be a very clear case of self-defense. Therefore, if I hear nothing to the contrary, the court will adjourn."

"Your honor! I object!"

Everyone twisted around and Glen saw Howard Trimmer. He wore a black suit and held a white stetson in his big gnarled hands. His voice was emotion-charged and Glen saw from the twist of his mouth he was about to explode.

"Yes, Mr. Trimmer, you have an objection. By all means speak up."

"I sure will," Trimmer rasped. "It was my men those two snakes killed. They were simple hard-working cowhands spending their pay and minding their own business when Collins arrived looking for trouble."

"Mr. Trimmer," Judge Bonner said. "There is a room full of witnesses who say differently."

"The hell with that! There ain't no way Collins could have beat Chase Lawson to the draw. Everyone knows he's no good with a gun. I say he had to have killed Chase with a hideout. Then he probably had a couple friends shooting from the upstairs rooms. That's the only way he could do it." Trimmer slammed his hat to the floor. "It was murder!"

A babble of voices erupted and Judge Bonner rapped his gavel for silence. "Shut up!"

The room quieted. "Now," the judge asked, "did anyone present clearly see Mr. Collins draw? I don't mean think they saw it, but would swear they did."

A man from the back of the room stood up. "I reckon I did as well as anyone. There was a couple of us hunched down by the window. But it was kinda dirty and they was standing pretty far back."

"Tell me what you saw," Judge Bonner demanded.

"Well, I ain't quite sure. Everyone was pushin' and shovin' to see and then it all happened so fast it was hard to follow. Chase Lawson was firing towards us and I just tried to get out of the way. Next thing I know, this man come flying through that window and he was dead before he hit the sidewalk. Hell of a mess with the glass and all."

"I'm sure," the judge replied. "It sounds to me like no one really witnessed Mr. Collins draw."

"Of course they didn't," Trimmer spat. "'Cause he can't!"

"Hmmm," the judge mused. He glanced sideways at the court clerk. "Give this man his pistol after you unload it."

The clerk walked over and handed Glen his gun and holster.

"Put it on, Mr. Collins. This is rather unusual, but you

say you outdrew one man and independently shot and killed two more. I want to see with my own eyes, as I'm sure everyone else does, if it was possible."

Glen stood up. He glanced over at Roy, then at Hap. Both men nodded and Glen felt better. He buckled the gun on and tied the holster down to his thigh. He flexed his fingers. The room was so quiet he could hear himself breathe.

"Are you ready?" Bonner asked.

"Yes, your honor."

"Then face Mr. Trimmer and draw on him."

Trimmer's mouth gaped open. "Now wait a minute, Judge. Empty or not I don't like this!"

"Very well," the judge said. "But you're accusing this man of murder and I want you to have the best view. Mr. Collins, face the bench and draw when ready."

Glen revolved forward. What if he dropped the gun? What if his thumb missed the hammer?

"Just take it easy," Roy whispered. "Do it like I showed you."

Glen nodded. He looked up at Judge Bonner and then he went for it. His hand shot down, not with Roy's speed, but very fast. The gun came up and he cocked the hammer all in one smooth and fluid motion. The hammer dropped loudly. The entire thing took place in scarcely more than a double eye blink.

The judge sat immovable and stared down the gun barrel. Finally, he seemed to rouse himself. "If either of you two men do anything like this again without it being self-defense, I'll send you to prison."

He studied Glen for a long moment. "You may put your gun away, Mr. Collins. I've seen enough. Case dismissed!"

CHAPTER 7

When the judge's gavel dismissed the courtroom, Glen found himself surrounded by a crowd. People shook his hand and congratulated him. Not surprisingly, Roy Winslow also found himself a celebrity. The two men's eyes met for a brief instant and Glen saw Roy laugh as someone said something into his ear.

Glen searched for Maria and finally located her standing alone and watching him. She winked and he felt good. There was pride in her face and Glen knew it was for him.

"Let's celebrate!" someone yelled.

"Yeah," another echoed. "To our next sheriff, Glen Collins!"

The crowd began to exit the town hall and Glen felt hands pulling him. He'd wanted to talk to Maria first, but realized that was impossible. He waved and called, "See you later!"

She nodded and Glen felt himself being carried by the crush of bodies out the door. At that moment, he felt as if he had everything in the world. Nothing would stand between himself and becoming San Diego's first sheriff, and no one, not even Roy Winslow, could steal the love of Maria Silvas.

Maria was almost the last person to leave the town hall. It had been a great day for Glen Collins and she lingered, savoring his victory. She knew there would be many toasts and congratulations. The death of Chase Lawson meant Howard Trimmer's plan for gaining control of San Diego was ended. She hadn't realized it before, but the town's celebration of the court decision was an expression of relief.

While it was true the people could have voted for Glen Collins, they might have been afraid to. Because Glen was a quiet man, unassuming and modest, they did not know of his strengths.

In the course of her reporting, she had often heard the view that Glen Collins was a good blacksmith—but sheriff? Never. He was too easygoing and not nearly good enough with a gun to protect himself, let alone the town.

Now they knew differently. With their own eyes they had seen his draw and even she had been amazed at the speed of his hand.

"Maria?"

She looked up quickly and was surprised to see Roy Winslow standing alone beside the door. The habitual smile was gone and she had the feeling something was wrong. She moved forward to help. It was because of Roy Winslow that Glen was alive. They had spoken only once, but she'd instinctively turned to Roy for help. He hadn't failed her. She would not fail him.

"What is it?" she asked. "Why aren't you over celebrating with the others. You are also a hero today."

His mouth curled with sarcasm. "It's Glen's party, not mine. And I never could stand playing second fiddle to anyone."

"Second fiddle?" The expression was foreign to her, but the tone of Roy's voice was unmistakably bitter. "Señor Winslow, what . . ."

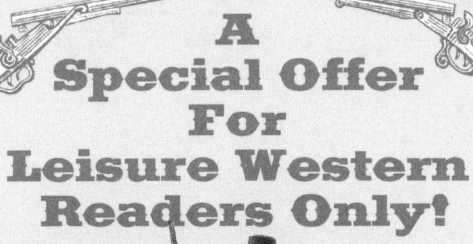

A Special Offer For Leisure Western Readers Only!

Get FOUR FREE* Western Novels

Travel to the Old West in all its glory and drama—without leaving your home!

Plus, you'll save between $3.00 and $6.00 every time you buy!

EXPERIENCE THE ADVENTURE AND THE DRAMA OF THE OLD WEST WITH THE GREATEST WESTERNS ON THE MARKET TODAY... FROM LEISURE BOOKS

As a home subsriber to the Leisure Western Book Club, you'll enjoy the most exciting new voices of the Old West, plus classic works by the masters in new paperback editions. Every month Leisure Books brings you the best in Western fiction, from Spur-Award-winning, quality authors. Upcoming book club releases include new-to-paperback novels by such great writers as:

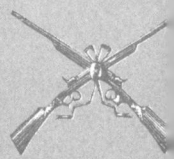

Max Brand   Robert J. Conley   Gary McCarthy   Judy Alter
Frank Roderus   Douglas Savage   G. Clifton Wisler
David Robbins   Douglas Hirt

as well as long out-of-print classics by legendary authors like:

Will Henry   T.V. Olsen   Gordon D. Shirreffs

Each Leisure Western breaths life into the cowboys, the gunfighters, the homesteaders, the mountain men and the Indians who fought to survive in the vast frontier. Discover for yourself the excitment, the power and the beauty that have been enthralling readers each and every month.

SAVE BETWEEN $3.00 AND $6.00 EACH TIME YOU BUY!

Each month, the Leisure Western Book Club brings you four terrific titles from Leisure Books, America's leading publisher of Western fiction. EACH PACKAGE WILL SAVE YOU BETWEEN $3.00 AND $6.00 FROM THE BOOKSTORE PRICE! And you'll never miss a new title with our convenient home delivery service.

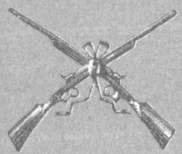

Here's how it works. Each package will carry a FREE* 10-DAY EXAMINATION privilege. At the end of that time, if you decide to keep your books, simply pay the low invoice price of $13.44, ($14.50 US in Canada) no shipping or handling charges added.* HOME DELIVERY IS ALWAYS FREE*. With this price it's like getting one book free every month.

AND YOUR FIRST FOUR-BOOK SHIPMENT IS TOTALLY FREE*! IT'S A BARGAIN YOU CAN'T BEAT!

LEISURE BOOKS   A Division of Dorchester Publishing Co., Inc.

GET YOUR 4 FREE* BOOKS NOW— A VALUE BETWEEN $16 AND $20

Mail the Free* Book Certificate Today!

FREE* BOOKS CERTIFICATE!

YES! I want to subscribe to the Leisure Western Book Club. Please send me my 4 FREE* BOOKS. Then, each month, I'll receive the four newest Leisure Western Selections to preview FREE* for 10 days. If I decide to keep them, I will pay the Special Member's Only discounted price of just $3.36 each, a total of $13.44 ($14.50 US in Canada). This saves me between $3 and $6 off the bookstore price. There are no shipping, handling or other charges.* There is no minimum number of books I must buy and I may cancel the program at any time. In any case, the 4 FREE* BOOKS are mine to keep—at a value of between $17 and $20!

*In Canada, add $5.00 Canadian shipping and handling per order for first shipment. For all subsequent shipments to Canada the cost of membership in the Book Club is $14.50 US, which includes $7.50 shipping and handling per month. All payments must be made in US currency.

Name_____

Address_____

City_____ State_____ Country_____

Zip_____ Telephone_____

Tear here and mail your FREE* book card today!

If under 18, parent or guardian must sign. Terms, prices and conditions subject to change. Subscription subject to acceptance. Leisure Books reserves the right to reject any order or cancel any subscription.

Get Four Books Totally FREE* – A Value between $16 and $20

Tear here and mail your FREE* book card today!

PLEASE RUSH MY FOUR FREE* BOOKS TO ME RIGHT AWAY!

LeisureWestern Book Club
P.O. Box 6613
Edison, NJ 08818-6613

AFFIX STAMP HERE

"Roy," he corrected roughly. "Drop the Señor. You don't say Señor Glen."

"Glen and I have known each other for years. We are very close . . . friends."

"Friends!" Roy laughed. "You have a strange way of putting it, Maria. I doubt Glen would approve."

Maria felt anger beginning to rise. What was bothering this man? Today, of all days, he should be celebrating his freedom. She searched his face and their eyes locked and held. Maria felt her breath shorten. There could be no mistake. She dropped her gaze.

"Maria, could we go for a walk? Like the evening we first met? There are things I want to say."

"I should," she said carefully, "get back to the newspaper."

"Please," he insisted. "It doesn't have to take long. I just want to talk to you."

She couldn't refuse this man. She owed him the life of Glen Collins. But it wasn't just that—there was something magnetic about Roy Winslow that she found almost irresistible. "All right," she heard herself say.

"Good!"

Together, they slipped out the back door of the town hall and passed quietly through the streets until they reached the edge of the town. They didn't touch or speak, but Maria knew the young man beside her had things he needed to say.

"Can we go farther, Maria? Unless you are tired. We could climb the hill and then rest. I imagine the view of San Diego and the harbor would be beautiful."

"It is," she said. "All right, we will go a little higher."

They stopped several hundred feet below the first crumbling walls of the presidio. Maria took a deep breath. She tasted the ocean breeze and watched the great sailing ships that arrived from all over the world.

Russia, France, England, and Spain—land of her ancestors. There were moments, like now, when she wished she could stow away on those ships and see other parts of the world. But that was a fantasy.

"Maria," he said, almost as though he could read her mind. "Have you ever left San Diego?"

She turned away from the ships. "Yes, I've been to Los Angeles and, once, when my mother was alive, we all went to Santa Barbara."

"Then you haven't seen anything. Not really. You should travel. Those beautiful eyes of yours would grow round with wonder at the great canyon in Arizona or the towering Rocky Mountains. There are deserts that shimmer in the sun and forests and rivers waiting to be seen and experienced. Surely you'd like to see them."

"Yes," she answered. "But I love this town of my birth. And my father, he needs attention and love."

"You have a life of your own to live," Roy said. "Someone as alive as you are shouldn't be content to hide themselves from the world."

"Hide myself?" She laughed softly. "I don't understand. I have everything I need here. My father, friends, and a job I enjoy very much."

Roy took her by the arm and Maria felt herself being pulled into his embrace. For one moment, his lips found hers, she resisted, then suddenly she realized she wanted to kiss him. The world stood still for a moment. Maria's eyes closed. It was a kiss like she'd never known and she might have wished it never to stop, but then she felt his hand begin to slide down her dress and over her hips.

"No," she cried, breaking free.

"Maria. I won't hurt you, Maria. I'm sorry. I don't know what got into me."

"Of course not," she said coolly. "It is time to go."

"Not until I'm finished with what I came to say," he replied. "Maria, I think I love you."

She froze. "We have only just met."

"I felt that way the first moment I saw you."

Maria shook her head, her eyes returned to the ships. "Roy," she began, "I have never known a man, only been kissed by a few."

"And never by one like me," Roy whispered, coming very close. "That's what I'm trying to tell you. In your mind, Glen Collins is something special. But he's not. He doesn't know anything."

He took her arm. "Maria, listen to me," he pleaded. "All I want is a chance."

"No," she whispered. "I am . . . a little afraid of you, Roy. You are wild and will not stay."

"That's not true! I want to make San Diego my home. I'm tired of roving. And today, in court, I really listened to what Judge Bonner said about this town's first sheriff and making a page in history. Maria . . . Maria, I'll prove it. I'm going to oppose Glen for sheriff!"

She stood on the hillside and couldn't think of anything to say.

"Maria," he said at last. "I want you to understand my reasons."

"I do, Roy. You want me and you think only Glen stands in your way."

"Well," he demanded, "isn't it true?"

"Perhaps," she whispered. She looked up, wanting to make him understand. Wanting to say how she felt. "I thought I loved Glen, before you came. Maybe I still do. You are both so different and I find myself thinking of first one, then the other. I don't know how I feel anymore."

She shook her head, trying to gather her thoughts. "What I am sure of, is that I won't let you destroy Glen."

"Destroy!" His face clouded darkly. "I'm not trying to destroy him. In fact, I like Glen Collins, believe it or not. I like him enough to know he's better suited to being a blacksmith than a lawman. Glen is running for sheriff because of you, Maria. That kind of motive could get him killed!"

"Don't say that," she whispered.

"It's the truth and you know it."

It was only a half-truth, Maria thought. She remembered Glen telling her of his wanting to make a contribution. And despite what Roy said, she knew that Glen had steel and heart enough to be a fine lawman. And from what she'd seen in the courtroom it was obvious enough that he could handle himself.

"My reasons are less flattering but a whole lot more honest," Roy said, breaking through her thoughts. "Judge Bonner was right, there ought to be ten good men running for that office. The least I can do is to see that there are two. I . . . I need you, Maria, but I also need the responsibility of that office. Up to now, I've never thought much of anything but myself. This could be my chance."

The way he said it, Maria sensed he was speaking from the heart. She had no illusions about his past. Roy Winslow had been a *pistolero* and a man on the run. No matter how good he was with a gun, knife, or women, Maria understood that sooner or later he would die swinging from a rope or facedown in a saloon. She looked at the man and felt an obligation. He needed her approval, his black eyes begged for it.

"Roy," she said, taking his hands in her own. "If you need to do this for yourself, I wish you success. Have you told Glen, or your brother?"

"No," he said quickly. "I'm not ready for that. Josh won't approve; he thinks I'm always looking for trouble and he doesn't want that in San Diego. What he'd really like is have me go into a nice little business and slowly die of boredom."

"I can't believe that," Maria said.

"Don't misunderstand. He wants the best for me. It's just that what he considers a 'fine opportunity' doesn't match with what I'd like to do." Roy smiled woefully. "That night when you raced in, we were starting to argue. He was trying to push me into opening a men's clothing store. Can you imagine that! Roy Winslow measuring the length of someone's leg for pants! Kneeling and scraping everytime the front door opened and someone walked in. I'd almost rather stay in jail."

"There are other things. Surely you could . . ."

"What?" he blurted. "I can't stand being cooped up, which means opening a store is out. I'm no good with figures and I spend money as fast as I latch onto it. Josh and me, we're just opposites. There's only one thing I can do well, and that's handle a gun or smooth talk people. Seems to me I qualify for sheriff on both counts."

She reached up and placed her hands behind his neck. Then she pulled him close and kissed him. For a moment, he did not respond, then his arms tightened around her and Maria felt his lips crushing her own. At last, she broke away and smiled. "That is for good luck. I wish you and Glen could both be sheriff."

He nodded. "Maria, do you love me yet?"

"No," she said happily, "but you are nice to kiss."

Roy laughed, and Maria, for some reason, felt like laughing too. Then they started back.

The day of the fiesta Glen quit work early. He picked up an armful of boxes at Wallach's Store and headed back for the livery. He could hardly wait to try on his new outfit. During the past few days he'd seen Maria, but only in spare moments. She was also excited about the fiesta, probably more than he. Thank God, Roy taught me how to waltz and step to the *contradanza*, Glen thought.

As he hurried on down the street, he met Señora Estudillo. "What is it you have in all those boxes?" she asked.

"New clothes for tonight, señora."

She placed her hand on his arm. "I know you would have looked splendid in Jose Antonio's outfit, but you are too big. May I see what you have? Besides," she confessed, "I thought you might like to see our preparations. I have had my entire staff working for days."

Glen could not refuse the invitation. Besides, there was plenty of time. "Tell me," he said, "since the reason for these festivities is your anniversary, what was it like?"

"It was beautiful," the old woman said. "We were married at the Mission Santa Barbara just before daybreak. Candles were held by all and the ceremony lasted through the golden sunrise. That was the way it was done in those days, to start a new life together with a new day."

"It must have been quite an occasion."

"The biggest wedding in California for many years, Glen. After the ceremony we had breakfast and then the entire party left for town. In Santa Barbara, we filled the streets in a grand procession. It was led by the presidio's military band and they were dressed in bright red jackets trimmed with yellow cord. Their pants were white and cut smartly in the Turkish fashion."

The old lady gazed into the distance and her eyes seemed to look back in time. "Jose Antonio swept me up and bore me to a carriage streaming with ribbons. Then, the band began to play and the procession began. Those not in the party itself cheered from the streets and fired their guns in salute as we passed; we traveled like royalty through the town, laughing and waving at the onlookers."

"And that night," she continued, "the entire population of Santa Barbara gathered on the hillside at the mission and everyone danced to the violin and guitar. When Jose Antonio and I waltzed, they stopped to watch and some threw silver dollars and the children cast roses at our feet. We danced all night with the musicians begging to take turns. We did not go to bed, Jose and I, until the next morning—and then only to make love. And that day, they held a feast, which was given by the father of the church."

"Were there a great number of people then too?" Glen asked.

"Even more. They came from the ships in the harbor and the ranches in the Santa Ynez Valley. Everyone was invited, old and young, the rich and the poorest. Mission Indians and some from as far as San Francisco. They did not leave the table hungry. The fathers had tables that reached from room to room and even more under the vine-covered verandas. And on every table, the food was piled high. Beef, pork, and lamb from the coal pits, cheeses, crackers, fruits, and barrels of wine and *aguardiente*. We feasted and danced for five days and nights."

Glen shook his head in wonder. "Five days and nights?"

"Yes," she replied. "By the third day the town people were so tired they did not go home at night but slept on the grassy hillsides until their spirits and bodies brought them back for more. On that fifth night the food and wine at last were gone. Jose Antonio asked me if he should send for more, but I said no. I was tired, and we wanted to be alone."

The story was over and the señora led Glen into the courtyard, and Glen saw that she had ordered a large, raised dance floor to be built near the fountain. Everywhere, people were hurrying with last-minute preparations. The courtyard was totally enclosed and covered on the front and both sides by a veranda. Underneath the veranda, tables were being filled with food and drink. Across the courtyard Glen could smell bread baking in the outside *horno*, or domed brick oven. Children were climbing the trees and hanging oil lamps. Everything seemed in confusion.

"Don't worry," the señora said. "By sunset, all will be ready. Now, come inside and let me see your new outfit."

He followed her into the grand *sala* and once again Glen was reminded of the splendor of La Casa de Estudillo. In one corner of the room was an elegant Steinway piano. Over a doorway was a statue of the Black Madonna of Monserate and nearby was a Duncan Phyfe sofa upholstered in the deepest blue Glen had ever seen. The floors were covered with oriental rugs and overhead hung massive ormolu chandeliers.

"Place them over here," she said, pointing to a great walnut table.

One by one, Glen opened the boxes to the delight of Maria Estudillo. The old señora smiled with approval when he held up the fine silk waistcoat and matching black vest. Next he unwrapped a white linen shirt, corded with lace at the cuffs. He wasn't sure about the pantaloons. They'd seemed a little too fancy but Roy had insisted. They were emerald green, made of broadcloth and split up the sides of the pantlegs below the knees. Strips of gold braid edged the splits and the stitching was elegant.

"Bravo," she cried. "I did not know you had such a taste for color."

Glen flushed. "I don't," he admitted. "Roy Winslow picked these out for me. I just paid for 'em."

The señora cocked her head sideways and gave him a curious glance. "He did this for you? Why?" —

Glen refolded the pantaloons and carefully replaced

them in their box. What was the value of telling her about Roy and what he wanted? It didn't make much sense and he doubted she'd understand. "He . . . he just wanted to help me," Glen said lamely.

"That is very interesting. I would not have supposed such a thing."

"Why not?" he asked suddenly.

She smiled. "No reason. Now, what are in the last two boxes?"

Glen turned back to the table. The señora hadn't wanted to answer his question. Did she know something, or see something she was unwilling to reveal? "There are my boots," he said absently, "and in this box, my hat."

As a final touch, almost ceremoniously, he put on the flat-brimmed hat. It was reddish-brown, made of vicuna wool imported from South America and the hatband was a row of silver eagles. "Do you like it?"

She clapped her hands in appreciation. Whatever had been bothering her was gone. "It is dashing! You will be the most handsome man at the fandango."

"Thank you, señora," he said gratefully. "I need all the help I can get tonight."

She moved forward and touched his cheeks. "You have done well and your appearance will make Maria proud."

"Do you think so?"

"I know so. And do not worry about a man such as Roy Winslow. True, he is dashing and has a way with words, but you have other qualities he may lack. I think Maria will come to see this, Glen. But right now she is confused and flattered by so much attention."

Glen swallowed hard. "What's going to happen?" he asked.

"I don't know. But I have great faith in Maria Silvas. I never had a daughter, but if I had been so blessed, I would want one like her. She will make the right choice.

Have faith. And be prepared to match this young man in Maria's eyes. A woman loves to be courted."

When Glen left, he thought about those words. Señora Estudillo was a very wise lady. Tonight, with his new clothes, he and Maria would waltz and do the *contradanza*. Then she'd see. Then she'd see.

CHAPTER 8

Glen placed the flat-brimmed hat carefully on top of his head and turned. "Well, what do you think?"

Hap swore softly. "If I hadn't seen it with my own eyes, I'd never believe I was looking at my boss, Glen Collins. Maria is going to have to beat the other women to keep 'em away from you."

"That," Glen chuckled, "don't seem likely. But you think she'll like it?" He was fishing for reassurance and knew it. If only, he thought, I can make a big impression on Maria. Everything counted on it and maybe, later, he'd even ask her to marry him. And why not? He was the town hero and the sheriff's job was as good as his own. He'd shown the people he could handle the job, and tonight he'd also show them that he could look and act like a man they'd be proud to elect.

He gave a final, nervous tug on his hatbrim. He owed plenty to Roy Winslow. If there was any way possible, he'd make it up to the man. After he wed Maria, perhaps the hard feelings would pass. There were plenty of other pretty women in San Diego; Roy wouldn't waste much time getting to know them once he understood Maria was taken.

"Hap," he said.

"Yeah?"

Glen set his jaw. He was going to do it. "I want to show you something." He reached under his bed and dug around until he found a small paper box. He reverently placed it on the bed and untied the cord that bound it.

"What's that?" Hap asked quietly.

"It's my Mom and Dad," Glen replied. "It's all I ever had from them." He looked up at his friend. "You never asked and I never offered, but my folks were killed in Nevada by the Paiutes. I was just five years old when they left me with friends. Had to leave Winnemucca and go to Reno."

Glen felt his throat tightening. He opened the box and gazed at the small ring. The ring was gold with a center-set ruby. Four tiny diamonds were placed, two on each side. None of the stones were large, and Glen knew the ring wasn't particularly valuable, except to himself.

"It's a pretty thing," Hap said gently. "I'm right glad you got something like that to remember her by."

"Hap, I've decided to give it to Maria tonight if she says she'll marry me."

Hap let out a mountainman holler. "Yahoo!" He jumped to his feet. "Sure she will! Congratulations!"

"Hold on, hold on," Glen laughed. "She hasn't said yes. She might even turn me down." But even as he said it, Glen felt good. Tonight he was going to put on a show. Not only that, but even after they were married he'd make her proud.

"Hey up there, we need help," a voice called.

Glen shoved the ring into his pocket. "Wonder who that could be?"

"We'd better go down and find out," Hap grunted.

They descended the ladder and Glen saw three men standing beside their horses. He recognized them instantly as riders for Howard Trimmer. "What do you want?" Glen asked, his voice tight and unfriendly.

They had a bottle of whiskey and were passing it back and forth. "My horse spooked at the tie-rail. Busted his bridle all to hell. Need another."

"I haven't got any for sale."

"You must have 'em hanging all over the place, Collins. We don't want a new one."

"Sorry. I'm fresh out of bridles today."

There was a silence as the three men seemed to digest the information. Glen saw them glance at each other, then pass the bottle around. Finally, one growled. "Is that our next sheriff? Don't hardly look like him to me. Don't even smell like him. We musta made a wrong turn."

Deep down inside, Glen felt a cold knot of anger growing. "You made a wrong turn, all right. Get out of here before I throw you out."

"Sounds real tough, don't he, Whitey?" one snickered.

"Sure does. I kinda liked the blacksmith that dressed and smelled like a pig better. Say, do you know what happened to him?" Whitey asked.

Glen drew his gun. The hammer cocked loudly and the man with the bottle to his mouth strangled on his whiskey. "Don't shoot!" he choked.

"He ain't going to shoot," Whitey laughed mirthlessly. "Judge Bonner would send him to prison for sure."

Glen studied Whitey. He was about thirty and his hair was the color of dried bones. Long and stringy, it hung from under his hatband. Glen stepped in on him but the man held his ground.

"Like a pig? Is that what you said?"

The eyes flicked down to Glen's six-gun pointing at his stomach. He nervously licked his lips and took a deep breath. "I forgot, Collins."

"I see." Glen lowered his pistol and then dropped it into his holster.

Whitey grinned. "Seems to me," he said, backing away slightly, "I do remember saying . . ."

Glen didn't wait for the man to finish or to get set to draw. He lunged forward, his fist whipped up and slammed into the man's jaw. Whitey crashed into his horse and bounced to the ground.

"Hold it!" Hap yelled. "You two are covered."

Glen pivoted on the other men. His expression was icy. "Come on," he gritted. "Either one of you. Better yet, both. Say something—anything!"

The two cowboys glanced sideways at each other. Neither one of them seemed inclined to accept Glen's offer. After a long hesitation they grabbed Whitey by the arms and roughly hauled him to his feet. Whitey's legs didn't seem to want to hold his weight so, together, they boosted him up and laid him across the saddle.

One turned back and grabbed the horses' reins. "Mister," he said, "Whitey is damned sure faster with his gun than Chase Lawson ever thought about. If I were you, I'd go to that fiesta tonight and dance with a tied-down gun."

"I'll do that," Glen promised.

"I just hope I'm around to see the day when you ride north and come across Howard Trimmer's land."

They mounted then, and Glen watched the two men ride away, leading Whitey draped across his saddle.

Hap Hazard holstered his weapon. "You better get going or Maria will be worried. I think I'll stick around a few minutes just to make sure they don't come back."

"They won't," Glen said. He rubbed his knuckles. "I hit that one hard enough to take the fight out of him tonight."

"I hope so," Hap said. "Sure wouldn't do to have him spoil the fiesta."

When Maria opened the door, Glen forgot about Howard Trimmer and all the trouble that seemed to be brewing like a storm. She wore a full dress of silk with a white Spanish mantilla that was breathtakingly beautiful against her black hair. The dress was scarlet, trimmed with white lace, and reached to the floor. But it was Maria who exclaimed her surprise and delight the loudest.

"Glen!" she whispered, her eyes round with unconcealed admiration. "The clothes, they are splendid!"

"You approve, then?" he asked in mock seriousness.

"Oh yes! You look very handsome."

Glen bowed. "And you, señorita, will make the moon and stars blush with envy."

Her eyes danced with delight and Glen knew it was his best line yet. He saw pinkness come to her cheeks and she seemed . . . actually dazed by his manner.

"Shall we go?" he asked, offering his arm. Then, before she could answer, he kissed her. Kissed her in a way that a man kisses a woman he wants and loves. Their lips met, their bodies came together hard, and Glen felt her passion rising to match his own. She did not seem to want to stop, but at last, it was he who gently broke free. "Listen," he said, "the violins and guitars have started to play."

She gazed into his eyes. "I hadn't noticed," she whispered. "Glen, what has happened to you tonight?"

He smiled. "After the dance, I'll tell you."

On the way to the fiesta, Glen felt as though everything in the world he'd ever wanted was about to come true. They talked little, only once and that was about her father. He learned that Juan Francisco had insisted on putting the final touches to the silver-mounted saddle. It was almost finished; he would join them at the fiesta before midnight.

When they entered the courtyard, Glen saw an enormous crowd. The night was warm, lanterns swayed from the trees, and the scent of flowers sweetened the air. Señora Estudillo had hired three guitar players and two violinists, and already, many of the guests had finished eating and had begun to dance.

He saw Roy Winslow, conspicuous with his sombrero, gracefully waltzing with a pretty young woman Glen didn't know. Glen felt a moment of defeat as his eyes watched them. Roy was already the center of attention and his movements were as fluid as those of a mountain lion. He turned to Maria and saw that she was also watching Winslow.

"Would you like to dance?" he asked.

She looked up quickly. "Do you want to?"

Why not, he decided. The sooner I get it over with the better I'll feel. He nodded and they started toward the dance floor. On the way, several people spoke to him but Glen only half listened. He was trying to remember the steps that Roy had shown him at the jail. They reached the edge of the dancers and stopped.

"Perhaps we'd better wait until the next dance begins," he hedged.

She nodded.

"Glen! Maria! Let me look at you."

He turned and saw Señora Estudillo standing beside them. "I have been waiting for you. Glen, you were the first to be invited and the first I shall dance with tonight."

Glen extended his hand. "With pleasure, señora."

Once on the floor, his bravado began to crumble. He wasn't sure how to begin and started on the wrong foot. There was a moment of panic and then the señora whispered. "I suspected as much, Glen. You have danced little."

There was no use in trying to hide the fact. Glen shook

his head in discouragement. "I'm sorry. I . . . I was hoping to do better. I guess we should set this out before I hurt you."

The señora's arm tightened on his shoulder. "Nonsense!" she said urgently. "This is the reason I insisted on the first dance. Before the next song is over, I will have you dancing as smoothly as your rival, Señor Winslow. Now, relax and follow me."

The señora was wrong. Actually, it took three dances before he began to get the swing of it. Roy had taught him the basic steps but practicing alone was an altogether different thing from dancing with a partner. Glen concentrated so hard he scarcely heard the music. Please, he thought, don't let me tromp on this grand lady! One misstep and I'll break her foot.

The floor was crowded. Around them, dancers swirled gracefully and the music played on.

"Evening," Roy called happily.

Glen looked up to see Winslow swing by with Maria. Damn, he raged and, missing his step, momentarily lost his balance.

"Pay attention!" Maria Estudillo hissed. "Never mind him. He is only trying to make you angry."

"Well he's doing it!" Glen rumbled.

A pair of bodies came wheeling through the dancers. Glen caught a sudden glance of Hap Hazard and a very fat Mexican woman, then they crashed.

"Whee-haw!" Hap roared. "Sorry about that! Señora Estudillo, save me the next dance. Hear now?"

Glen had just managed to pull the señora away from the couple before they struck. The collision had almost knocked them off the upraised floor into a flower bed. "Fool," he gritted.

The señora laughed. "See, you thought you were the

only one with troubles tonight. But I have the next dance with him!"

"I'll have a word with Hap first," Glen promised.

"Thank you," she replied gratefully. "Now, we have only a few moments until this dance ends. Then you must dance with Maria."

"I don't think I'm ready," he said. Through the mash of dancers, he watched Roy and Maria. How could he ever hope to compare?

"It is not so important how you dance," the señora said, as if reading his thoughts. "What is important is who you dance with. Remember that."

When the music ended, Glen and the señora found themselves near Roy and Maria. Glen nodded stiffly at Roy, then turned to her.

"May I have the honor," he asked gravely.

"Of course," she replied.

Roy tapped him on the shoulder and leaned close. "I figured you'd take this one. So I gave a couple silver dollars to the band." He almost laughed. "This dance will be the *contradanza!*"

At that very moment, the announcement was made and most of the couples left the floor. Glen felt sick inside. The *contradanza* was an intricate dance and involved paired couples who stepped in unison. Each would line up and, as their turn came, would move forward and spin to the right like a perfectly matched pair through the upraised arms of the next couple. The line clapped to the tempo and the movements were quick and precise. There was no room for error.

Roy grabbed a partner and the line formed. Without realizing it, Glen found himself and Maria at the front. Hands began to clap and the music quickened.

Glen took a deep breath and looked at Maria. Her face was excited. Before he could speak, she took his hand and jumped forward. Glen stumbled, tried to remember the steps. Toe and heel, bow, raise the arms and wheel to the right just as Roy had taught him.

Suddenly everything seemed to go wrong. He threw his arms up and spun into the next couple almost knocking them down. An apology rose in his throat and, before he could react, the second couple in line jumped out and he twisted to avoid them. What was wrong! This wasn't the *contradanza!* Go to the right. Toe and heel, bow . . .

He slammed squarely into a dancer, tripped over another and fell. The music stopped. The entire courtyard became silent and Glen wished with all his heart he could just shrivel into nothingness.

"Maybe you better sit this one out," Roy laughed. He grabbed Glen by the arm and tried to pull him up.

Glen threw the hand off. He balled his fists. There was just one thing he wanted—a piece of Roy Winslow! The man had duped him, knowing Glen would make a fool out of himself. Well, he'd succeeded. All the high hopes, practice, clothes, dreams, they didn't mean anything now. Everyone saw him for the fool he was. Should have stayed in the barn where he belonged.

Glen shook his head with bitterness.

Suddenly, Maria was on her knees beside him. He looked up and saw her eyes were glistening, her face set and white. "Glen," she whispered. "What happened? Why did you try to dance the *contradanza* without knowing the steps?"

He couldn't tell her the truth. All he had left was his honor. "I . . . I must have been thinking of another dance, Maria."

She nodded, looked up and when she spoke her voice was knife-edged. "Play a waltz," she ordered.

The music started and Glen stood, hunting for Roy Winslow. The man was already beginning to dance. Glen saw Señora Estudillo and the old woman seemed to be pleading with her eyes. No trouble.

Glen felt Maria take his hand. He scarcely noticed so intense was his desire to strangle Roy Winslow. The decision was clear enough. He could go after Winslow now and ruin the fiesta mood, or he could wait until it was over and meet Roy afterward. His choice. The señora was nodding at him across the dance floor. Glen's shoulders sagged; he would wait.

Glen brushed off his clothes, mumbled apologies to the other dancers, and took Maria in his arms. He could still waltz and he wanted everyone to know it. He forced a smile. "Don't worry," he said. "I'm not going to fall down or step on you."

"I know. I saw you dancing with the señora. You were doing very well."

Glen nodded his thanks and they began. Maria danced as lightly as a cloud. As the evening wore on, Glen began to feel better. Dancing with such a woman would make any man feel proud. She seemed to have forgotten about the *contradanza* and Glen, looking into the deep pools of her gaze found himself enthralled. She was a stunningly beautiful creature, sensual, graceful, lithe, and strong. Glen felt that her eyes seemed to read what was inside him and, somehow, find it good and right.

Finally, the band stopped for a short rest. Glen and Maria were talking to Josh Winslow and his wife when Roy suddenly stepped upon the musician's stand and pulled his gun. He fired twice and all heads jerked in his direction.

"Excuse the interruption," Roy called shoving his gun back into his holster. "But I have an announcement to make."

"What's he up to, Maria?" Josh asked.

Maria bit her lip. "I'm not sure."

"The announcement has to do with the recent trial at

which many of you were in attendance. As you know, my brother, your mayor, has served San Diego well these past years."

Glen heard Josh groan, "Is he crazy!"

"I have," Roy continued, "only been in this city a short time. But already, I feel at home among you."

There was a scattered clapping of hands.

"Anyway, those of you who were at the trial heard the honorable Judge Bonner say that there should be ten good men running for sheriff."

Glen felt his stomach tighten; he knew what was coming now.

"Well, I've been told that it's no fun watching a one-horse race. So . . . if you don't mind, ladies and gentlemen, I'm going to follow in my brother's illustrious footsteps and cast my sombrero into the ring."

With exaggerated flourish, he swept off his hat and sailed it high into the air. Then, before anyone could move, Roy drew his gun and fired four times, and at each shot, the sombrero skipped higher. The hat lit on a low-hanging tree branch and everyone saw the four bullet holes perfectly spaced around the brim.

"Well I'll be damned," a man swore. "Would you look at that!"

A roar of approval swelled and the spectators broke into applause. Roy Winslow shoved his gun into his holster and bowed. He stepped over to the tree and retrieved the sombrero. "Who wants a souvenir from your next sheriff?" he shouted.

A group of young ladies waved their hands excitedly, but Roy looked past them as though they weren't even alive. He was watching Maria.

A harsh sound spilled from Glen's lips. Roy had pushed him too far. Enough was enough.

"Don't!" A voice said quickly. "Don't you see," Josh

Winslow hissed, "he wants you to throw a punch at him."

"That's one wish he's got that's coming true," Glen rasped.

The hand tightened. "Glen, don't do it. You'll look like a fool. Let me talk to him alone. I promise you he'll listen!"

"He's right," Maria said quickly.

Sure they were right, Glen thought. But did it really matter any longer? Roy Winslow had humiliated him tonight and used the fiesta as a stage for his own play. Glen saw the faces of the crowd. And as Roy sauntered toward Maria, Glen knew that those same faces were watching him. They were waiting to see just how far the dashing newcomer to San Diego could push their blacksmith. The sheriff's election was no longer a one-horse race.

Glen planted his feet on the floor and pushed Maria aside. It was the wrong thing to do, but he couldn't help it. When Roy stuck out the bullet-stitched sombrero, Glen figured he'd make him eat it.

Roy was almost there, but his smile was gone and he wasn't looking at Maria any longer. The two men measured each other and, around them, the crowd separated.

Two shots. If the musicians had been playing, they wouldn't have reached their ears. But in the silence of the impending confrontation, both shots seemed very loud. They came from down the street.

Glen forgot about Roy. He pivoted on his heel and charged out of the courtyard. As he rounded the corner of San Diego Avenue, he saw the dim shapes of three horses pounding away into the night. Twenty yards farther, he skidded to a stop in the street and felt his insides go hollow.

Juan Francisco Silvas lay stretched, half in, half out of his saddle-shop doorway. Even before he reached the man, Glen knew Maria's father was dead. And he knew the murderers.

CHAPTER 9

Glen knelt beside Juan Francisco's body. There were two bullet holes in his chest and it was obvious that he'd died instantly. Maria's father had been as well liked as any man in San Diego. Glen shook his head disconsolately. Why? The old saddlemaker owned nothing of value and kept no money. Then, almost as the question came, he knew the answer.

He picked up Juan and carried him inside. Gently, he laid Juan on a table and removed his new waistcoat and draped it over the body. He didn't want Maria to see her father like this. Glen studied the room, slipped the toe of his boot across a pool of blood. He bent and picked up a leather knife and wiped it clean. So, he thought, Juan hadn't died without a fight. Somehow, he must have managed to strike before he was killed. Was it Whitey with his pale, bloodless eyes and chalky hair? Or one of the others? It didn't matter, Glen thought bitterly. All three would hang.

He studied the room quickly, looking for anything that might reveal what had happened. There wasn't much else to see. Apparently, they'd taken Juan Francisco by surprise.

Most likely, he knew, they'd come for a bridle and their eyes hadn't been able to leave the silver-mounted saddle.

Glen could almost picture how they must have stared at it a long time. They'd have passed the whiskey back and forth a few times and maybe even glanced at several proffered bridles. But somewhere between the bottle and the goods that Juan presented, they'd made their decision.

Glen closed his eyes and a great feeling of remorse passed through his long body. If he'd have sold them a used bridle, maybe this would never have happened. They'd have simply left town and Juan would still be alive. Guilt, as terrible and as crushing as a mountain slide, drove at him and Glen shuddered under the weight of it. Why hadn't he forced Whitey to make his play? Instead, he'd sent three dangerous men straight to the only place in town that was open where a bridle could be found.

He whirled and started for the door. He couldn't bring the old man back, but he sure would see that justice was carried out and Juan rested in his grave—avenged.

At the door he saw Maria trying to break free from Roy Winslow's arms. She was fighting him savagely.

"Let her go," Glen ordered.

Roy turned her loose and Maria swept past him and ran into the saddle shop. Glen stood back. He saw her fingers come to her lips. A small cry like a wounded animal came out. For a moment, he thought she might faint and he stepped closer.

She swayed, then he saw her gain control, seem to find some deep reservoir of strength. He witnessed a new part of Maria that he'd only suspected, and one that made him love her all the more.

She looked at Glen, her eyes wet and glazed with pain but intent and searching. "Did anyone see who killed him?" she breathed.

Glen hesitated, aware that Roy Winslow was also listening. "No," he said finally. "I saw three men gallop away but the light wasn't enough to identify them."

"They killed him for the saddle, Glen. It was sitting right over there," she pointed with a shaking finger.

He reached up and took her hand. "I know, Maria. When I find the saddle, I'll have the killers."

He looked past her and saw Hap Hazard standing by the door. Hap's face was like an iron mask, brittle to the point of shattering. The old hunter and Juan Francisco had been good friends; they'd spent many hours together swapping stories. Hap's gaze locked with his own and Glen read the message. They both knew the killers, and they knew where to find them. Time was being wasted.

"Maria," Glen said softly. "I have to go now. Hap and I will find them, but we must go quickly before they get too much of a head start."

Maria clenched her fists at her side. "Yes, we must hurry!"

She started to brush by and he stopped her. "You can't go," he said. "Maria, you must stay."

Her eyes flamed defiance. "No!" she cried. "I am going. You are not yet sheriff or my husband and you have no authority over me."

Her expression was uncompromising, her chin set with grim determination. She wasn't hysterical and she wasn't anything less than dead serious. Glen knew he was whipped.

"All right," he sighed. "Hap and I will meet you at my livery. We'll pack some provisions just in case. Change clothes and get your horse."

"And a gun," she said evenly.

He nodded. "All right, a gun too. We leave in a half hour."

Roy stepped forward. "I'm coming along. Like Maria says, you don't have the authority to stop me."

"I don't want you, man. Do you understand?"

"Sure," Roy said. "You see this as your big chance. Catch those three murderers and you're the hero who gets elected, not me. And in Maria's eyes you're . . ."

Glen swung open-handed; his palm cracked into Roy's face and rocked him backward. Like a snake, Roy's hand streaked to his gun and the hammer went click. Glen froze and felt a chill sweep through his body as he stared down the gun barrel. Roy's expression was pinched and mean. A trickle of blood ran from a split upper lip and dripped down upon his shirt.

It was probably less than ten seconds before Roy seemed to gain control and lowered his gun, but to Glen it seemed like ten years. He'd been on the very brink of extinction, and somehow been saved. He'd watched as Roy's whole body seemed to fight and shudder for reason. Pearl drops of sweat covered his body, and Glen's legs felt weak.

"You ever do that again, you're dead," Roy breathed.

"Sooner or later," Glen replied, "it's bound to happen. This town won't hold the both of us, Winslow."

"That means whichever one of us loses the election had better fog it out of San Diego," Roy said. "I don't want to go to prison for killing you. That's the only reason I didn't pull the trigger just now."

They both heard Hap's gun uncock. "You were covered, Winslow," he graveled. "You're damn lucky I figured you wouldn't shoot."

He stepped between them. "Glen, I feel the same way as you do, but if the trail leads where we figure, we're going to need his gun. Think about it, and Maria."

Glen didn't like it. He wasn't at all sure what Roy would do in a gun battle. He'd seen a wild madness in the man's eyes a moment ago that still left him feeling unnerved. But they did need Winslow's gun—desperately.

"All right," he conceded, "as long as you understand that I intend to bring those three men back alive if at all possible. They'll stand trial and their judge will be Bonner, not you or me."

"Agreed," Roy said flatly. "Now suppose we stop wasting time and get out of here."

The moon was almost full under a cloudless cobalt sky as they rode their horses at a gallop out of town. Before leaving, Glen and Hap had made their plan. The three killers were on Howard Trimmer's payroll but it couldn't be assumed they would head for the Trimmer ranch. As powerful as the cattle baron was, Glen knew he wouldn't be fool enough to have sanctioned the theft or murder.

No, Whitey and his partners had acted on their own whiskey courage. Even now, Glen thought, the three men were probably beginning to sober and realize their mistake. And one of them would be in pain. Glen wondered how bad a stab wound the man carried.

Another thing they'd soon realize was that the silver-mounted saddle would be all the evidence needed to hang them. It would attract comment and attention no matter how far or fast they traveled. Glen figured there was only one thing they could do—strip the saddle bare and ditch it, taking only the silver.

They'd still hang. The silver was as clearly marked as coin. Every piece sculpted and designed for exact placement on the saddle. Their only chance then, was to melt the silver down. But that took special equipment and skill —and time. Glen figured to catch them first.

Hap Hazard was a frontiersman and a tracker. He immediately picked up the trail going north, but then lost it on El Camino Real, the King's Highway, which traveled north to Los Angeles.

"Too damned many tracks," he grunted. "Can't separate them."

"They're bound to stick to the road a couple miles," Glen said, "before turning off."

Roy twisted in his saddle. "What makes you so sure they won't stick to it all the way to Los Angeles?"

"Because," Glen answered. "This is too well traveled, even at night. It's over a hundred miles to Los Angeles and somebody would spot them for sure. Three men dressed as working hands with one hurt and another carrying in a silver saddle would arouse anyone's suspicion. Remember, they didn't have time to change saddles and we haven't seen an extra one yet."

"O.K.," Roy said sullenly, "so they're on the road now but not for long. Where does that leave us?"

"In a tough spot," he admitted. Glen considered the problem, turned it around in his mind and studied all angles. He told them about his hunch that the trio would have to hide long enough to pry the silver loose and ditch Juan's saddle. One of them might need rest from losing blood. It seemed pretty certain, then, that they'd have to take cover before daylight and get as far away from the road as possible. At least that's what he'd do if he was in their boots.

For the first time since they'd started, Maria spoke, but her words were strained and forced. "I agree. But that still doesn't tell us which way they will take. East into the hills or over to the ocean."

"Maybe I'm wrong," Glen said slowly, "but I'd say they'll head for the beach."

"I disagree," Roy snapped. "If I was being chased I'd ride for the high ground. Hell, there's enough sycamore and oak on those hillsides to conceal an army, let alone three men!"

"Let's ask Hap," Maria said, eyeing the two younger men. "This is no time for you two to begin arguing."

Hap mounted stiffly. He looked back down at the tracks and shook his head. "One of the horses we follow is fresh shod. I can still see the nail-head marks. But there are at least thirty separate tracks made in the last day."

"Quit jawing and answer the question," Roy spat.

"Easy boy," the old man said, "or I might just have to cut out your flapping tongue before this is over."

Hap didn't wait for the outburst. "I'd say go west alongside the road until we discover where they turned off."

"The hell with that!" Roy charged. "I'll cover the eastern side of the road."

"Suit yourself, sonny."

Hap's easy acceptance seemed to make Roy less confident. He gazed up at the dark rolling hills that bellied down to the coastline and finally shook his head. "If you know something I don't, maybe you ought to say it out plain. Or perhaps you'd prefer I ride up there alone and get ambushed. Is that it?"

"Señor Winslow," Maria flared. "I will not stand for that!"

In the moonlight, Roy's expression went hangdog.

"So it's back to señor, huh? All right, señorita, I apologize. But I think those two owe us some kind of explanation as to why they're so certain the men we follow are going to head for the Pacific."

The request was legitimate and Glen knew Roy deserved an answer. "It's the saddle," Glen said. "They haven't got a shovel and they couldn't find a cave in the dark. There's only one place where no one could ever find it."

"The ocean," Roy said, nodding slowly.

"That's right. Besides, they could ride along the surf

for miles and never leave a track. And there's hundreds of small coves and grottoes they could hide in by day."

"Another thing," Hap interrupted. "Those hills are soft and grass covered. This time of morning the dew is heavy. Come daybreak, we'd be able to follow their trail as easy as if they were plowing through snow."

Roy chuckled dryly. "All right, I give up. If they're as smart as you are they'll go west."

Glen nodded. "Then let's start riding. They've got better than an hour's head start."

Whitey Upton cursed silently as he waited for the two men to catch up. They were in a hell of a mess and there didn't seem to be an easy way out. What made things worse was that Howard Trimmer would hold him personally responsible. Bill Singleton and Rafe Dockins were just saddle bums. They could be disposed of later. But what really bothered Whitey wasn't killing the saddle maker or the posse that was following. No, the thing that made Whitey sweat fear was how his boss, Howard Trimmer, would act.

The old man's orders had been very simple. Ride into town, come up with some pretext to visit the Blackhawk Livery, then try to force Glen Collins into a gunfight with the other two as witnesses. There'd be another trial, and the big rancher hadn't tried to hide the fact that Whitey might be sentenced to prison. But if he could have gotten Collins to draw first, the prison sentence wouldn't have been long and Trimmer's lawyers might even get him off scot-free.

Whitey had been in prison seven of his thirty-two years. He hadn't found it that bad—hell, for ten thousand dollars he'd take a couple years behind bars standing on his head. Bill and Rafe hadn't known about the deal. All they'd been interested in was a night in town and the fact that Whitey was doing the buying. Problem was, he'd bought them too much whiskey. The moment those two had seen the silver-covered saddle they'd gone for it. Rafe had slugged the old man and taken a knife wound in the shoulder. Then, before Whitey could stop it, Bill had opened fire and grabbed the saddle.

He shook his head with disgust as he heard their horses approaching. He could have stopped it, but who'd have believed him? Juan Francisco was dead and neither Bill or Rafe would have told the truth. So feeling trapped, he'd had no choice but to run. Damn, he thought, how can I get out of this mess without Trimmer nailing my skin to the barn?

Rafe was bent over his saddle and even with just the moonlight, Whitey could see his face was drawn and the color of candle wax.

"You going to make it?" Whitey asked.

"Hell yes," Rafe gritted. "But I'm losing blood, man!"

"Hang on," Bill grunted. "Once we get back to the ranch, Mister Trimmer will send for a doctor."

"No," Whitey heard himself say. "We're not going back. Not yet, at least."

"What do you mean!" Rafe gasped. "I need doctoring."

The beginning of a desperate plan took hold of Whitey. It wasn't complete, but he had the start of it. "Use your heads. If we ride back with a posse on our heels, Trimmer ain't going to help any of us. Fact is, I ain't at all certain he wouldn't kill us first. You know as well as me how Trimmer wants to be a big man in town. He spent a lot of money backing Chase Lawson before the fool got himself killed."

"Who cares about that," Rafe swore. "I'm bleeding to death!"

Bill Singleton scratched his jaw. "Wait a minute, Rafe. Whitey is right. He knows Trimmer better 'n we do." He glanced across the distance between them, and Whitey watched the instinct for self-preservation at work. "What are we gonna do?"

Whitey had that one figured out. "We're going to hole up somewhere until we can sort this thing out." He motioned to the silver saddle Bill carried on his lap. "We need to get rid of that."

Both men jerked erect. Rafe, sweat beading on his face gritted. "No we don't. If Trimmer won't stand up for us, this saddle will buy our way free. Must be at least a thousand dollars worth of silver on it."

Bill Singleton hugged the saddle closer. "I go along with Rafe. We killed a man for this and it's too late to change things now."

"Fine," Whitey shrugged. "Just see how far you get carrying that saddle around. It's the evidence that'll hang all three of us."

He let them think about it before going on. He rolled a cigarette and the silence grew. Finally, he said, "Boys, we might as well carry a sign around as that saddle. We'll be pushing up grass before a week goes by."

"Well, what do you suggest?" Bill asked.

"Think," Whitey said. The answer was so obvious even these two fools would get it. But it was important they arrive at the solution on their own.

"We could pry the silver loose!" Rafe cried. "Get rid of the saddle and keep the silver."

Bill rubbed his hands across the leather, his fingers traced the silver work. "Yeah," he said slowly. "I thought of it too. Only . . . only I just hate to do it. I never seen anything I admired so much."

"Cut it out!" Whitey spat. "Is it worth dying for? And even if we could take it with us, what then? The damned thing would attract so much attention no one would even want to buy it from us. Look close, you fool. See the saddle maker's stamp? As if he needed one!"

Bill nodded sullenly.

"Let's quit jawing," Rafe moaned. "I need help."

Whitey swiveled around in his saddle. "We can't be more than an hour ahead of them. Just up ahead is a stream that runs to the ocean. I say we ride down it to cover our tracks. When we get to the beach, we travel north through the surf until we find a cove. We can hole up there tomorrow and pull that silver loose. Come night, we throw the saddle off a cliff into the ocean and head for Los Angeles."

"I could die before then," Rafe whispered.

"No you won't," Whitey said. "I've done my share of patching up knife wounds and bullet holes. There ain't nothing better in the world for sucking out poison than fresh seaweed."

"That right?" Rafe asked. He sat up taller and his face pleaded for hope.

Whitey grinned with his lizard-thin lips. "Sure is, Rafe. And the bleeding will stop just as soon as we do. By tomorrow morning, you're going to feel a whole lot better. Especially when we divide up all that silver."

The man forced a chuckle that sounded to Whitey more like a rattling sound. "Then let's go," he wheezed. "I don't know how much farther I can ride."

"It won't be far," he promised. "There are places back under the cliffs big enough to hide a herd of cattle."

Just as he'd promised, they came to the stream and splashed their way toward the ocean. Whitey rode in front and when he reached the Pacific, he reined north. Behind them, the waves swept away their hoofprints and Whitey kept his eyes on the shoreline. Up ahead, he could see the high sandstone cliffs marching right up to the ocean. Fortunately, the tide was out and they'd not have to swim. But in a few hours, they'd be locked in when the tide rose and no one could reach them. That's what he wanted, some time to work out a plan. A plan of escape that wouldn't include Rafe or Bill Singleton. Not that they weren't still useful. Somehow, he knew, he'd have to use those two as a decoy. A sudden thought came to his mind.

"Hey, what you stopping for?" Bill asked.

"My cinch. Feels loose. You and Rafe go on ahead, I'll be along in a minute."

Bill nodded and rode by. As they passed, Whitey peered at Rafe. The man was almost unconscious. Bent over in his saddle desperately trying to hang on. In the moonlight, Whitey saw the glistening blood on his shirt. Rafe wasn't going to be able to stick it out much longer. They'd have to find a cove soon. After all, Whitey figured, a dead decoy was no decoy at all.

He waited until they were a couple hundred yards ahead. Then he rode his horse out of the water and up onto dry sand. He went far enough to where he was certain the waves would never reach. Then, he dismounted and checked his cinch. When he finished, he climbed back into the saddle and rode directly into the water.

He chuckled to himself. Glen Collins would find the tracks but he'd never understand why. No, the big fool wouldn't even suspect Whitey's intent. A hunter only used a decoy when he wanted to attract the animal he hunted.

The roles were switched now, Collins would go for the bait and die. It was the only way Whitey could think of to square things with Howard Trimmer and he knew it would work.

CHAPTER 10

They had reached an impasse, and Glen knew it was time to gamble. Overhead, the stars were fading and it was almost daybreak. Hap Hazard squatted on his heels in the road and examined a cigarette butt. Glen's nerves were as taut as wire, but he remained silent, waiting for the old man to answer the question that was on all their minds.

"Well," Hap said finally. "They stopped here and must have palavered for a while. This cigarette butt still smells of smoke. But the tracks aren't as fresh anymore. We've lost a lot of time hunting their cut-off trail. I'd say they're about two, maybe three hours ahead."

Roy Winslow rode a wide circle around their group and reined back to listen. When Hap finished, he snorted with disgust. "All right, so they stopped and one smoked. They didn't turn off, so what are we waiting for?"

"Ease up," Glen said. "They must have reached a decision. I'd bet they'll be taking the first chance they get to head for the ocean."

Hap lit a match and crabbed across the dirt. He picked up a rock and held it to the light. "Look here. Fresh blood." His voice grew husky with emotion. "Good for you, Juan Francisco!"

Maria prodded her horse forward and they followed. Since they'd left town, Glen had been watching her closely. Several times, he'd tried to find words that might express his own sorrow for the death of Juan Francisco. But she hadn't given him any attention. He was worried about Maria Silvas. Maybe if she'd cried, or even tried to talk out her feelings, he'd have liked it better. But she'd kept it all locked inside. Riding through the night, she had sat stiff in the saddle and her eyes had never once left the road. What was she thinking? Was it only revenge? Or was she reliving the past, remembering Juan Francisco and how she'd loved him?

Less than a mile farther they came to the stream. There were many like it that flowed down from the verdant hills into the ocean. And every one would hide the tracks of the men that they hunted. But Glen was inclined to believe they'd choose this first exit. He reined his horse in and told Maria, Hap, and Roy that the trio would not want to risk meeting travelers on the road and, with every minute that passed, the chances increased. Also, one was badly wounded and needed rest. He said he believed they had to gamble and assume the men they followed had left the road here.

There was little argument, not even from Roy Winslow who seemed to have lapsed into a surly let-him-make-the-blunders attitude. Glen understood his reasoning. He'd been overruled at every point, and Roy was now content to let mistakes be made. And later, it would be Roy Winslow who would bail them out.

Glen guided his horse down the stream. His eyes scanned both banks but he knew it was wasted effort. Whitey had brought them this far; he wouldn't make any dumb errors now.

The stream fanned out on the beach and submitted itself humbly to the great ocean. The waves pounded, curled their foam at the sand, and at the very last moment, slapped meekly to rest. Then they pulled back, gathered, and assaulted the shore again. Over and over. Never tiring, they marched at the land. As he did every time he came to the ocean, Glen felt an overpowering sense of struggle. Maybe, he thought, mankind is a little like the waves—each generation building, throwing itself at life, then receding to be born again. The great ocean cliffs stood battered and worn. They held siege against the indomitable foaming armies that marched to strike again and again. Perhaps . . .

"Glen," Hap called.

He rudely pulled himself back to the present. This was no time to be mesmerized by the ocean. For just up ahead, three desperate men were seeking cover. Perhaps for refuge, but more likely for ambush. "Yes?"

Hap pointed and they all saw the tracks. A man had boldly ridden from the water and dismounted high up on the beach. Then he'd traveled back into the water and the hoofprints were gone.

Glen studied each member of the group, hunting for some answer. Even Roy Winslow wouldn't meet his eyes. No one, it seemed, could figure it out.

Glen dismounted. Just ahead was a rocky promontory that jutted into the ocean. They'd be holed up somewhere on the other side—waiting.

"What the hell are you doing!" Roy hissed.

Glen pointed up at the cliffs. "There's only one way we can reach them," he said quietly. "And that's by going around that point."

"Then let's ride!"

"Go ahead if you want. Course you'll have to swim your horse through those breakers. And if you don't get smashed on the rocks, you'll make it."

"Then that's the chance we have to take. What's the matter," Roy sneered. "You getting scared."

Glen let the remark go unanswered. At least two men

were waiting somewhere on the other side of those rocks. Maybe three if the knifed man was still alive. And Glen was scared. Scared of finding themselves caught out in the breakers totally defenseless and at the mercy of rifle fire.

He looked up at Roy. "Yeah, I guess I am. Seems to me, even if you could swim your horse to the other side, you'd find yourself drenched. Could be that gun you use so well might not be operating. In fact, I'd have to bet on it. And if they are waiting, I'd say your chances of reaching shore alive are worse than none."

Roy flushed. He turned on Maria for some hint of encouragement. Instead, she voiced anger. "Don't be a fool, Roy. Getting ourselves shot or drowned won't bring justice to my father's killers. It won't be long now before the tide goes out."

"But Maria," he protested. "We can't just sit here and wait. They might escape!"

"No," she said firmly. "They are as trapped as we are by the tide. Please, let us take rest and wait. I travel with three brave men. I do not wish to see anyone die foolishly."

A half mile to the north, Whitey Upton, Bill Singleton, and Rafe Dockins were trapped. They had passed the rocky promontory only to find that the cliffs were now much closer to the ocean and the beaches were no more than slivers of sand. The breakers thundered against the rocks, and before they'd quite realized it, there was no way forward or back.

Fortunately, the beach upon which they found themselves stranded was deep enough in one corner to keep dry even at the tide's highest point.

But it wasn't the cove they'd hoped for, and Whitey cursed the ocean. The tide was the one thing he hadn' reckoned on. But at least, he thought, Glen Collins and the others were as imprisoned as he was.

Whitey trudged down to the water and hunted up a pile of seaweed. He didn't really know if the weed would help Rafe or not. But it might. The Indians, he remembered, were always using some kind of root, bark, or weed as a poultice.

When he straightened up with the dripping seaweed, his eyes scanned the cliffs for a way out. It was obvious he'd have to go on foot. But he thought he saw a chimney in the rocks that might be climbed. His eyes followed it upward to the top. Yes, he could scale that wall and escape. And one thing seemed plenty certain, he'd better do it in the next few hours before the tide receded.

He tromped back up the beach and knelt beside Rafe. The man's cheeks were sunken and Whitey didn't need a doctor to tell him Rafe was on fire. He carefully unbuttoned the shirt and peeled it free. "Take this shirt down and wash it out," he said to Bill Singleton.

When the man returned, Whitey began to wash away the blood. The salt water splashed into the wound and Rafe cried out in pain.

"Easy," Whitey said, pushing him back roughly. "This has to be done. The wound is infected. The seaweed will draw it out."

At least, Whitey hoped it would. And the part about the infection was true. The knife had struck deep, just below the collarbone. Already, he could see thin tendrils of purplish lines radiating outward just under the skin. With all the blood Rafe had lost, Whitey didn't give him much chance of surviving. But whether or not Rafe made it wasn't important. As Whitey sponged the last of the blood away and pressed the seaweed to the wound, he was hoping for just one thing—to keep Rafe operating long enough to fight their pursuers.

"Ahhh! Oh God," Rafe screamed as the salt water hit the exposed nerve endings.

Whitey knocked away Rafe's clutching hand. "It'll feel better in a minute. You just lie here and rest. Me and Bill, we're going to have a quick look around."

The man was more alert than he'd expected. "No, you can't leave me!" His pain-glazed eyes blinked with fear. "Bill, don't let him leave me."

Bill Singleton looked away toward the ocean. "Don't worry, Rafe, nobody's going anywhere for a while. Rest."

The two men sauntered away and halted at the water's edge. Whitey cleared his throat and chose his words very carefully. "You know," he began, "we're in a tight spot."

Bill nodded silently; his face was bleak.

"But," Whitey continued, "we still have a good chance to get free."

"We do? How?"

Whitey pointed south toward the rocky point. "They'll have to come around that. No matter how long they wait, the tide won't go out that far. The water will still be up to their stirrups. It'll slow 'em down and we can pick them off as they come through."

"Maybe," Bill said, his voice lacking conviction. "Kind of depends on their size. If there's only four or five, we can shoot 'em out of their saddles before they reach shore. But if there's ten or twenty, we haven't a prayer."

"We might," Whitey said quietly, "if we got them in a cross fire. They'd have no cover."

Bill looked up quickly. "Spell it out, man! You got something in mind, let's hear it."

"O.K., I think I should try and climb out on foot."

"The hell with that!" Bill raged. "You talked us into this mess and you're not going to run now!"

Whitey had an urge for killing. And if his plan hadn't included Bill Singleton, he'd have shot him right then and been done with it. But he roughly curbed his fury and said, "Listen, you and Rafe were the ones who drilled the saddle maker. Not me! You were drunk and not thinking."

"It's done! You'll hang as sure as us."

"No one is going to hang if you'll just listen until I finish," Whitey spat.

"Go ahead," Bill said finally. "But you ain't running out on Rafe and me."

Whitey relaxed. "If I can get to the top, I can walk south until I'm over those rocks. When they come around, we'll have our cross fire. We'll pin them down on the beach and it'll be a slaughter."

"Me and Rafe, we won't have any cover either," Bill pouted. "The only one that will stand a chance is you. On top."

"Wrong!" Whitey protested. "It wouldn't take five minutes for us to dig a couple trenches in the sand. One for you and one for Rafe."

"The only trench Rafe needs is one about six feet deep," Bill said. "You know that as well as me."

Whitey's expression assumed defeat. "All right, let's level with each other. I got a half bottle of whiskey in my saddlebags. If we pour some down Rafe's gullet, he'll last long enough to handle a rifle. Between the two of you down in a trench resting your Winchesters, you ought to be able to pick off your share. Under fire, they'll break and try to escape. That's when I go to work. I'll make sure what's left don't retreat around those rocks."

"I dunno," Bill said. "But I guess it could work."

"It has to. Listen, if we don't kill them all, every damned one of them, they'll wait us out until more arrive or they send men up there." He pointed to the top of the cliffs. "If that happens, we're as good as finished. They could pick us off at will."

Bill nodded. "But there's just one thing I ain't sure of."

"What's that?" Whitey asked cautiously.

"How do I know you won't reach the top and just keep going?"

There it was, the question he'd been dreading. Whitey took a deep breath and looked squarely into Bill Singleton's eyes. "Two reasons. The first is that Glen Collins knows I was in on it. So if Collins lives, I'm still a wanted man."

"Not good enough," Bill replied. "You could leave this country and never be found."

"The second reason," Whitey continued, "is that I'll be on foot and they'd run me down."

"Maybe," Bill answered.

"All right," Whitey blurted, "there's one other reason that should convince you. There's the saddle. Once we strip its silver there's a lot of money, and if Rafe should die . . ."

He'd let his words trail off knowing full well that Bill would get the drift.

"You're a no-good bastard," Bill chuckled.

All at once Whitey knew he'd won. He laughed openly and slapped the man on the back. "Like you said, Singleton, Rafe ain't gonna make it and half a share is better than a third."

"True." Bill's eyes narrowed. "But we keep the silver down here on the beach. You can have yours when you come back."

Whitey pursed his lips and frowned. "No trust," he muttered. He paused as if weighing the alternatives. Finally he shrugged in defeat. "Aw hell, you win. Let's go back and cut that silver loose, then dig your cover. It's going to take me fifteen or twenty minutes to make the top and I want to have enough time to scout up a good vantage point for firing."

"Yeah, I'll second that," Bill said. "And you just keep

thinking about all that silver. I want you to shoot your best."

"I will," Whitey said. "I damn sure will."

They were ready less than fifteen minutes later. Bill and Rafe had both positioned themselves in shallows and their carbines rested squarely on covering piles of sand. Bill Singleton had suddenly decided they should wait to remove the silver from Juan Francisco's saddle until after the showdown. Inwardly, Whitey laughed. Bill was afraid of him. Didn't trust him at all.

The man knew he couldn't pack the saddle up the cliff; the silver was his insurance. Whitey dug into his saddlebags and found the whiskey. Rafe needed it bad. The morning air was damp and cold but Rafe's face was bathed in sweat. "Rafe," he said, "when this is over we're heading for a doctor. But first, you got to help us. Drink some whiskey. It'll steady your aim and make you feel better."

Rafe smiled weakly. "Always has," he breathed.

Whitey nodded and stood erect. It was time to go. "Bill, I'll be waving when I get to the top. Just remember you got all the advantages. They'll be in the ocean and let them come until they're nearly to shore. Then we'll both open fire. They won't have a chance."

Bill swallowed noisily. He was scared but trying not to show it. "Quit jawing," he blustered. "I'll feel a whole lot better when you're on top looking down your rifle's sights. Damned if I can see how you're gonna make it up there anyway. Must figure you're half mountain goat."

Whitey grinned. "I can do it. Grew up in a Colorado mining town so I learned how to climb almost as soon as walk. So long, boys."

He came to the base of the cliff and started to climb. Over his shoulder he carried a lariat, one end was tied around his waist, the other knotted to the rifle. If he got into a jam he might be able to swing the rifle up into the rocks until it wedged. Then he could overhand himself up the rope. The carbine would take a beating, maybe even ruin the firing mechanism.

Whitey kept climbing. It wouldn't matter whether the rifle made it up the cliff or not; he wasn't going to need it. Once he made gain to the top, he was going to keep moving. He'd get another horse on the road and head for the Trimmer ranch. With any luck at all, Rafe and Bill would put a bullet into Glen Collins before they died. And that would just about wipe the slate clean.

It was time. Glen studied the waves and estimated that the surf was no more than five feet deep at the point. Their horses could make it without going off their feet. That was critical because Glen knew a swimming animal would be knocked over by the waves. A horse thrashing around underwater was dangerous. Only one thing bothered him. What if Trimmer's men waited on the other side? It would be a perfect setup. The possibility made him shudder. They'd be in the ocean and unable to move. The longer he thought about it, the more certain he became that it was a foolish risk. He peered sideways at Maria who sat with her arms folded on her knees staring at the water. Glen shook his head, thinking about how she could be fired upon when they rounded those rocks.

"Maria," he said. "I'm going to wade out there to the point and have a look. If it's clear on the other side, I'll signal. Hap can lead my horse."

She looked up suddenly and he knew her thoughts had been miles away. "When I was young," she said, "my father and mother used to bring me to the ocean. I always loved it. But this morning, it seems somehow cold and frightening." Her hand reached out and her fingers brushed his cheek. "Be careful, Glen. Now that my father is gone, I couldn't bear to lose you."

His voice was thick with emotion and he took her hand in his own. "Don't worry, girl. I'll be fine."

Glen removed his boots and shirt. Barechested, he shivered and knew the water was going to be very cold. He stopped by Roy and Hap and told them his plan. Surprisingly, Roy didn't protest. He just nodded stiffly. Glen couldn't shake the feeling that Roy was like a stick of dynamite and the fuse was smoldering very close to the powder. He'd have preferred the man to argue, or at least get angry. Anything but an uncharacteristic silence. Glen stepped by and yanked his Winchester from his rifle scabbard. Keeping it dry wouldn't be easy. He'd have to hold it aloft and hope it stayed operable.

The water was cold. Glen edged his way along at the base of the rocks, exploring the footing with his toes. The rocks were shiny with sea plants, and several times, he almost slipped. Mussel shells cut his feet and crabs scuttled for hiding. Each time a wave came in, he tried to climb up on a rock. Twice, he lost his footing and staggered, but never did the rifle go under.

The water was almost to his chest when he finally gained the point. Here, the depth was to his shoulders and Glen moved like a man in quicksand. He had to hurry or be smashed into the rocks. Back on shore, he'd observed that the breakers came in series. Three big ones, high and murderous, then a pause and several small, choppy ones. Unfortunately, the huge waves were coming. Glen had one final rock to move around before he had a clear view of the other side. He pressed his body as far up on the cliff as he could, then waited, counting as each breaker struck him in the back and tried to tear him loose. He clung there, hanging on the wet, slimy wall until the heavy waves shook back. Then he stepped down and plowed through the foam until he was on the other side. Where the south face of the cliff was almost vertical, the northward side was not. It was torn and crumbling; its base was strewn with great boulders and draped with kelp. Glen spied a rock just ahead. It was low enough to be climbed and he badly needed a place to rest. Stabbing pains flowed up through his raised arm; the rifle felt like he carried a tree. His feet were badly lacerated and every faltering step was agony. Rounding the point had been far harder than he'd expected, the waves and rocks had beaten him as no man had ever, even in his closest fight. He was almost there.

Something hit the water and plowed spray at his face. The second bullet was even closer. It struck a rock inches from his head. Glen's eyes swung to the shore. He saw a puff of smoke on the sand and heard the whip-song of another bullet. He lunged for the rock, lost his footing and knew he was going to fall. In a wild moment before his body went under, he threw the Winchester into the air praying it would land on the rock. Then he twisted and a wave bowled him under. The tremendous force of the water twisted him and hurled him against the jagged cliff.

A terrible pain ripped his side and he gasped. Salt water flooded his mouth and he gagged for air, flailing to reach the surface. His head emerged and he took a deep breath. A thunder filled the air and another struck. He just had time to brace himself against the cliff but then horrible tentacles of ocean kelp wrapped themselves about him. Terror filled his mind and he clawed at the slimy vegetation, tearing it away.

The third wave was the strongest and it flattened him on the rocks. Almost finished, he hugged the rocks with his entire body until the force, at last, subsided.

During the next minute, while he lay there sheathed in

agony, there was no more firing. The wave had thrown him into cover and it saved his life. He felt sick from swallowing the ocean and his strength was gone. But he had to move before the next series of waves. He pushed himself up and crawled higher. Glen forced down his sickness, willed away his pain. He had to get that rifle!

Slowly, keeping the boulder between himself and the shore, he inched upward until he was out of the water. Two more shots hit into the rock and Glen flattened. He waited five seconds, then scrambled up until he had the Winchester. He ducked out of sight and jacked a shell into the chamber. His eyes, bloodshot from pain and salt, blurred and he roughly heeled them with the palm of his hand. Now it was his turn.

He was so weak his arms trembled, so he rested the weapon against the rock and sighted. His first shot was wide, he saw it kick up sand. The second shot was dead center, but an instant later, the man popped up and returned fire. Glen swore to himself. They were going to be tough to flush out. Then he realized what there hadn't been time to notice before. Someone was missing! He saw three horses but only two men. A shiver of dread passed through his frame and Glen instinctively knew it was Whitey who was gone. Heart pounding, he glanced up at the top of the cliffs fully expecting to see the man. But even though he inspected every foot of the rim within his range of vision, he found nothing. It only made good sense. Whitey had set a trap and he wouldn't show until all his pursuers rode into view.

Glen took a deep breath. There was no alternative, he had to go in alone. There were enough rocks along the cliff to cover him all the way to the beach.

He began to move, leaping and rushing from cover to cover, hearing the bullets strike the rocks, returning fire, then dashing forward. It was treacherous work but it had to be done. At any minute, Roy, Hap, and Maria could decide to round the point. Roy was too headstrong to wait; if he heard guns, he'd come charging into the cross fire. Time was running out.

As he advanced, the hail of bullets increased its intensity. He was almost to shore now. The water was no higher than his knees. Glen crouched behind the rock and tried to evaluate his next move. He'd come as far as he could without being a clear target. Now, all that separated him and the two riflemen was forty yards of open beach. There wasn't a chance in the world he could cross that space alive, not with two rifles pointed his way.

All at once they opened fire and Glen ducked. He needn't have. Their bullets were directed toward the point. Glen didn't need to twist around. Roy, Hap, and Maria had ridden into the trap! Glen stepped out and began shooting as fast as he could. Then he leaped forward and charged. If he could flush them, rattle their aim —anything—it might give the others a chance.

He didn't charge straight in, but zigzagged. His long legs had always been able to cover a lot of ground in a hurry, but in the deep, clinging sand, he felt like a sleepwalker.

The rifles swung on him, like a pair of death fingers. Glen hit the sand and, in a split second, saw the face of the first man. He was shirtless and Glen was aware that he had blood on his side. They fired together and a bullet sliced Glen across the arm. But his own bullet scored. Glen saw the man slam over sideways and twist onto his back. Then he didn't move.

"Whitey! Whitey goddamn you. Now!" a voice cried.

Glen couldn't believe his eyes. Bill Singleton raised up on his knees, his face was contorted, alive with fear. He was looking at the cliffs above, and at that moment, he looked like a condemned man beseeching the heavens for mercy.

Glen jacked another shell into the chamber and took aim. But he couldn't shoot. Bill Singleton was beyond reason. He kept yelling over and over for Whitey; he'd given up the fight.

"Drop it!" Glen shouted.

Bill's eyes turned on him. Glen saw his lips move soundlessly. His own finger tightened on the trigger.

"Drop it, I said! You're under arrest."

Bill staggered to his feet, the rifle fell from his hands. Two shots. Glen saw them punch into Bill and drive him backward out of the sand trench. Then he grabbed his chest and screamed a final time.

A horse swept by and almost knocked Glen down. Roy Winslow's fuse had finally exploded the powder. The man jerked his horse to a standstill, his gun trained on the body. After a long pause, he saw Roy slump forward. He knew he hadn't missed. Roy's lips curled into a contemptuous smile and he holstered his gun.

A low growl erupted from Glen's mouth. In two strides he was beside Winslow's horse. His long, work-muscled arm swung up and grabbed the rider. With a tremendous heave, he yanked Roy Winslow from the saddle and hurled him to the beach. Before Roy could recover, Glen was on him, pulling him to his feet, slapping his face, forehand and backhand so hard it sounded like the far-off crack of lightning bolts.

Roy's eyes glazed, he staggered and seemed unable to resist.

"Glen, stop!" Maria cried, throwing herself between them. "He's been shot!"

Glen's hand, raised for another blow, froze in midair. He released Roy's shirtfront. Then he saw the darkening circle of Winslow's blood.

Roy swayed, his voice was no more than a whisper. "I'm gonna kill you, Collins."

"Go ahead," Glen said. "You just murdered Bill Singleton."

"Murdered?" Roy swallowed. "No, I saw him drop the rifle. Musta been out of bullets. He was going for his pistol."

"Uh-uh." Glen said. "He'd lost his nerve and was surrendering."

"That's . . . that's a lie," Roy gasped.

Glen trudged over to Singleton and picked up the dead man's rifle. He levered a bullet and pointed it at the sky, not taking his eyes off Roy. Then he fired. He repeated the process two more times, and at each, a nerve in Winslow's face twitched.

"I . . . I didn't know." He turned to Maria. "I swear," he pleaded, "Maria, I thought he was going for his gun!"

"Señor Winslow."

Roy staggered forward, reaching out for her. "Maria, that man was one of them that murdered your father. I thought he was going to kill Glen. You have to believe me. I did it for you!"

Glen saw her look his way. Then she turned back and he saw her straighten. "It . . . it was a mistake. An honest mistake, señor, you did what you had to do." Roy smiled weakly. "As long as you understand."

"Perfectly," she replied. "Now let's have a look at your side. There has been enough blood spilled. Come, lie down."

Glen stood at the shoreline waiting for Maria to finish bandaging Roy. Fortunately, it wasn't bad and had only traveled through the fleshy part of his side, below the ribs and above the hip. Glen watched the sea gulls chase each other over the waves or charge one another with quick movements on the wet sand. He didn't much care for them; they always seemed to be squabbling among themselves. The sandpipers were much better. They were all legs and bills and pretty much spent their time probing the sand for food. He looked back to the point. The tide was coming in now. They had to leave.

"Glen?"

"Yes, Maria."

"What now?" she asked.

"You know the answer to that. Whitey Upton escaped and I've got to go after him."

"Let him be," she said quickly. "Enough have died. There can be no more revenge."

He reached out and grasped her by the shoulders. "It hasn't been revenge for me. Your father and I were close friends and I won't try to say that I didn't want to kill when I first saw what they'd done. But now, I just want it over and finished. It's not finished as long as Whitey Upton is free."

She looked him in the eyes. "I love you, Glen Collins. Will you return to San Diego for me?"

"I can't," he said helplessly.

She nodded. "All right, then I am going on with you."

"Why?" he asked. "Because of your father?"

"No," she said simply. "Because of you. If you went alone, or took Hap, Mr. Trimmer might try and kill you. He wouldn't do that with a woman."

"Are you so sure?"

"Yes. I don't like the man, but I know he respected my father. He often came to the shop and bought things. My father never argued with Mr. Trimmer and he never raised his prices because of the man's wealth. He treated him exactly like any other customer and it seemed to mean something. I don't believe he would kill the daughter of Juan Francisco and that means safety for you also."

Glen smiled. "Sounds like you've pretty well thought this out."

"I have. And I'm riding wherever you go. You can't stop me."

"Well," he said, "then there's no sense even trying. We've got a pretty good distance ahead, let's get started."

They walked hand in hand on the way back to the horses. Hap had been busy. He'd taken the silver saddle and roped it down onto Whitey's horse. The two bodies were draped across their own saddles. It was a hell of a shame, Glen thought, that they hadn't been able to take Bill Singleton back to stand trial. There was only one witness left, and Whitey wasn't going to come easy. Hap was going to have to escort the injured Roy Winslow and the rest of the horses to town. He wouldn't like that at all. It was pretty obvious he'd prefer to leave Roy to fend for himself and head for the Trimmer ranch.

But maybe Maria did have it figured straight. Glen wasn't sure. He didn't want her in any danger and he sure didn't want protection, but if the big rancher would cooperate peacefully, they'd take Whitey back alive. That's the way Glen wanted it, but he couldn't help thinking it wasn't going to happen. Whitey had betrayed his friends so he could escape. Glen understood why Bill had cracked. The man had been expecting support and it never came. Whitey was a double-crossing snake and he'd sink his fangs into someone before he'd surrendered.

No matter what Trimmer did, Glen had the feeling he'd better keep his gun loose in the holster—it wasn't over yet.

CHAPTER 11

Glen Collins and Maria Silvas rode their galloping horses stirrup to stirrup as they crossed onto Trimmer land. And what a land it was! Verdant, rolling hills with grass lush and deep enough to reach the bellies of the cattle they passed. Crystal-clear streams glistened in the sun and raced from the higher country to the west, all churning toward the Pacific Ocean. They saw oak trees laden with acorns, blue elderberry, holly-leaved cherry, and big stands of western sycamore. Sea figs ripened on the branches and wild berries choked the ravines.

Why, Glen wondered, would a man with so much want even more? Howard Trimmer owned an empire in paradise, yet he seemed intent on extending his dominion over San Diego. Both Glen's and Maria's eyes constantly roamed over the hillsides, for they knew from past stories that Howard Trimmer kept outriders posted across his land to intercept strangers.

Yet, as the miles passed, they saw no one. It was as if Trimmer had pulled in all his forces and was waiting. For what, Glen thought cryptically? One man and a woman? If Trimmer was expecting a battle, he was going to be very disappointed. It would take no less than fifty seasoned fighters to mount any kind of challenge.

They topped a hill and there it was—the Trimmer

ranch. Both he and Maria reined in their horses to a standstill and sat motionless in their saddles.

"I'd heard about this place," Glen said, "but I never realized how big it was!"

"Like a city," she replied, "at least a settlement."

It was true. Glen saw the main ranch house, then barns, corrals, livery, what appeared to be a general store, and two long buildings he guessed would be the bunkhouse and dining room.

"Look!" Maria said pointing.

Glen nodded. He saw the smoke puff of a rifle and a second later the sound reached them. Almost at once, what looked like a small army of men emerged from the bunkhouse and fanned out across the buildings. And every one of them held a rifle. "Trimmer is expecting us," he said. "The welcoming party awaits."

Maria looked over at him. "We live or die together, Glen." She reached down and yanked her rifle out of its scabbard, then levered a shell.

"Put it away, Maria."

"No," she answered. "If they open fire on you I want them to know they must also kill me. There is one down there whose hands are stained with my father's blood. He must return with us."

"I thought you'd had enough killing."

"I have." She swallowed and gripped the rifle tightly. "But I've been thinking. Howard Trimmer would enjoy seeing you dead. After you become sheriff he will find a way. So . . . so we must face him now and get it over with. He is a danger that would hang over our marriage like a shadow."

"Our marriage?" A smile lifted the corners of Glen's mouth. "I haven't even asked you yet."

The tightness left her voice and she laughed. "If we are

successful today, you will. Already you have waited too long. Last night I saw the other single girls watching you. I cannot take the chance any longer. If you will not ask me, then I will ask you."

"What about Roy Winslow?"

Her chin lifted and she glanced away. Glen saw her face redden. When she looked back, her eyes were full of mischief. "He had you worried, didn't he?"

This was crazy! A half mile away a small army stood waiting to shoot them out of their saddles, and here they sat, Maria proposing marriage and him admitting his jealousy. At that moment, with the lazy blue sky above and death waiting below, Glen knew that, someway, they had to come through. But right now, Maria's question remained unanswered. "Yeah," he admitted, "Roy Winslow had me worried. Jealous as hell. He knows all about women and me . . . I'm pretty clumsy."

"Señor Winslow knows too much about women, I think," she said quietly. "I would not want to try and take the place of all those he has known and loved. Besides," she winked, "it will be more fun to learn together."

The way she said it and the vixenish smile on her lips made Glen want to reach over and haul her out of the saddle. They could make love in the tall grass. But there'd be an audience.

"We'd better get on down there," he said huskily, "before I change my mind."

She nodded, and her expression grew sad. "I've spoken . . . spoken very boldly, Glen. But I wanted you to know how I felt before we go on."

He took a deep breath and nudged his horse forward, unable to answer. Deep inside, he felt overwhelmed by her admission. But as they drew closer to the ranch, he also felt a deepening conviction that he and Maria would survive. They both had too much to live for to die this day.

"That's far enough!" Trimmer barked. "Where are the others?"

"What others?" Glen asked.

"The posse."

"There is no posse. Just Maria and myself."

Without a word, Trimmer gestured his arm out toward the hills. Instantly, four men sprinted for the corral and seconds later raced away. "Now, what do you want, Collins?"

"Whitey Upton." He stepped out of his saddle and strode over to face the rancher. "He killed Juan Francisco Silvas. He'll have to stand trial."

"Go to hell!" Trimmer spat. "I saw the last trial. Remember? Judge Bonner and the whole town are against me. There's no justice in San Diego. If there's anything to settle, it'll be done right here and now on my land." His voice lowered. "This time, I'll have all the witnesses and I'll be the judge."

"Señor Trimmer."

For a moment, they'd all forgotten Maria. But not now. Her rifle was up and pointed at Howard Trimmer's chest. Glen saw the rancher's face drain white.

Maria's voice was little more than a whisper when she spoke. "Two of your riders are dead. We would please like to have the third to stand trial for the murder of my father."

Out of the corner of his eye, Glen saw a movement "Hold it!" he yelled.

Maria's rifle pushed forward and they saw her finger tighten on the trigger. "Tell your men to drop their weapons, Señor Trimmer. Or you will be the first to die."

The way she said it left no doubt in anyone's mind Maria Silvas wasn't bluffing.

"Do as she says," Trimmer roared. "Nobody make a stupid move. That's an order!"

"Where's Whitey?" Glen demanded.

"How should I know?" Trimmer clipped. "Last time I saw him he was . . ."

Glen slapped Trimmer hard. A trickle of blood welled up on his lips. "Now I don't want to hit you again," he said deliberately. "But we aren't leaving without Upton. So, where is he?"

"You're pretty tough, aren't you," Trimmer rasped. "You'll make a fine sheriff as long as a woman backs your play."

Glen laughed but there was no humor in it. "That's really clever. Try to shame us into putting away our guns and then your fifty cowboys can step in and set things right. Uh-huh, Trimmer. No deal."

The rancher's lips curled with disgust. "I've broken better men than you with my bare hands."

"Maybe," Glen said, "but I doubt it."

"You're yellow, Collins. Yellow clear through."

"Oh hell," Glen muttered. "You win. Take your best punch, Mr. Trimmer. You won't get another."

Glen lowered his fists, saw a wicked gleam light Trimmer's eyes. For a second, the cattleman hesitated. "You mean it?"

"Sure," Glen said bracing his feet. It was probably stupid, and it was going to hurt, but he instinctively realized he had to gain the rancher's respect. There was too much gut in Trimmer to lose face before his men. Glen knew he couldn't slap it out of him—Trimmer was proud and he'd die before he talked. So maybe this was the only way. Glen stared evenly at Trimmer and saw his shoulder dip.

Trimmer was a mighty big man, standing almost as tall as Glen and weighing twenty pounds more. His gnarled fist swept in and caught Glen alongside the jaw. Glen's arms flew up and his feet left the ground. He struck the dirt and rolled feeling the world spin. He shook his head and spit blood. His entire face felt numb. Somehow, he clamored to his feet. "That was . . . was your best punch?"

Trimmer rubbed his knuckles and studied Glen. The meanness was gone. "Yep," he said, "that was as good as I got."

Glen reached into his mouth and dislodged a molar. He held it up and drawled, "Well, Mr. Trimmer, your best punch is pretty damn good. Now, would you kindly tell me where we can find Whitey Upton?"

The rancher stepped closer. His voice slipped so low that no one else could hear. "And if I refuse?"

Glen dropped the tooth. "Mister," he breathed, "if you refuse, I'll have to show you my best punch."

The man rubbed his jaw reflectively. "That," he said, "I'm not anxious to see."

"And I'm not anxious to show you. But we won't go back to San Diego without him. Whitey killed Maria's father. Juan Francisco was a good man. A damned good man! I kind of thought you felt the same way. Now, it's your move."

Trimmer pivoted and barked an order. "Tell Whitey to come out."

A minute later, Upton emerged from the bunkhouse. He was wearing his gun and Glen noticed that he kept his hand very close to the holster. But Glen wasn't watching his hands, not yet. It was the man's face that held his attention. Whitey was going to strike and no one, not even Howard Trimmer, could stop him.

"Whitey, I know what I told you but I want you to go back to town."

"No! You promised," Whitey growled. "I told you how it happened. I'll hang if I go back!"

"No you won't," Trimmer replied. "I'll get the best lawyer in . . ."

"You old fool! Don't you understand? There's no witnesses to say I didn't do it. We was all three in the saddle shop!"

Trimmer recoiled. He wasn't used to being spoken to like that. But even so, Glen had to admire the way the rancher stayed under control. "Whitey, give me your gun," he ordered.

Whitey's mouth opened and shut like a trash-fish out of water. They all saw his chest expand and heard him exhale. "I'll give it to you, Trimmer," he giggled. "I'll give it to you good!"

Glen knew what was coming the second he heard the laugh. Hatred? Fear? Whatever, Whitey had been pushed too far. Glen saw the hand streak for the gun. He dove forward and crashed into Trimmer as the first shot blanketed the stillness. Glen's pistol was in his hand as he fell. Whitey fired once more, intent on killing Howard Trimmer. Then, before he could turn his gun on Glen, Glen's own weapon was bucking solidly in his hand. At the same instant, he heard the heavy boom of a rifle. Whitey Upton was blown off his feet. His gun coughed a final bullet into the sky and he was dead before he struck dirt.

Maria was off her horse before the echo died off the hillsides. She raced to Glen. "Are you all right!" she cried.

"Sure," he smiled. "But you better look at Trimmer. I think he might have been hit."

Before either of them could move, a crush of men grabbed them.

"Stop!" Trimmer bellowed. "Let 'em be!"

There was a welt of blood over the rancher's left ear. "Just a scratch," he said. "Doesn't hurt half as much as my backside where you knocked me down."

"Sorry," Glen said.

"Damn, boy. I've been knocked over by a horse easier. Give me a hand up."

Glen did and Trimmer stood on his own feet though he looked wobbly. His eyes slowly appraised Glen, then he spoke to Maria. "I guess I was wrong about your boyfriend."

"Many have made the mistake of underestimating him. We must go into the house and bandage this wound, Señor Trimmer."

"Ahh, it'll be all right."

She took his hand. "Please, come with me."

Glen had to smile as he watched them walk toward the house. Big Howard Trimmer followed Maria like an oversized puppy. Glen pivoted around and stared at Whitey Upton. Then he bent over the man and it was almost a full minute before he stood erect and ambled thoughtfully to the ranch house.

It was the end of a long day. Glen, Maria, and Howard Trimmer sat on the porch and watched a brassy sun slide down to rest. He'd wanted to ride back to San Diego, but Trimmer had insisted they stay for dinner. Now, with glasses of cognac, Glen felt almost human. He'd taken a brutal pounding from the ocean and a purple discoloration shadowed his jaw line. But they were alive. His eyes traveled across the ranch yard to the hill where he and Maria had faced up to the likelihood of death and the promise of a life together. It seemed to him it had happened a lifetime ago.

He knew their lives would never be the same and, perhaps, neither would Howard Trimmer's. Gone was the ferocious intensity that had become his trademark. Maybe the bullet wound alongside his head made him think how close he'd come to being killed. Almost as though he read Glen's thoughts, Trimmer leaned forward and refilled their glasses. "You saved my hide, Collins. I've been si ting here trying to figure out why. Not a single reason comes to mind."

"I'm not sure myself," he admitted.

Trimmer frowned. "You know, I've had my share of grief. I once owned a plantation in the South. They took it away from me after the war. My wife and sons bled and died building a spread in Wyoming before I came here." He looked Glen straight in the eye. "I'm not asking you to understand why I operate as I do, but I've found a man has to take what he wants. And that's only the start . . . maybe the easiest. Once he's got something, like this ranch for instance, he has to fight every day just to keep it. All my life I've been scraping and clawing. It's the only way I know how to operate."

Glen nodded, sipped his drink. "I can understand that, sir. But things are changing. It's up to the law and the courts to mete out punishment or reward. If I become sheriff, you won't see me taking the law into my own hands. It wouldn't be right. And if someone tries to take your property—or your life—it'll be my job to stop 'em."

"Like with Whitey Upton. Is that what you're telling me? That why you did it?"

"Yeah," he said. "I guess it is."

Trimmer digested that. Finally, he stood up and stretched. "It's been a long day but a valuable one. Maria, I'm mighty sorry about what my boys did to your father. I hope you believe I knew nothing about it. Juan Francisco was a craftsman and I liked him very much."

Maria looked up. "I believe you."

Trimmer hesitated, seemed unsure of himself. "I appreciate that," he said softly. "And some way, I'm going to try and make it up to you."

"You don't owe me anything."

He touched the bandage on his head. "Maybe not, maybe so. Glen, I'll be leaving you two alone. I imagine you've got things to talk about." He started to walk away, but paused at the front door. "You'll make a fine sheriff. I'll back you all the way."

When the door closed, Glen chuckled, "Can you believe that? Yesterday he wanted me dead and tonight . . . tonight he says he'll back me."

Maria smiled and came over to sit in his lap. "You're our man, Glen Collins. We both know you'll make a fine sheriff."

"I haven't won yet. There's Roy Winslow to beat and I got a feeling he didn't pack those bodies down a side street. No siree. Unless I'm all wrong, he returned to town a hero this afternoon. Wounded, bringing in the killers. Hell-fire, Maria! The whole town is probably celebrating and Roy will be the main attraction."

She snuggled closer. "Maybe, but tonight, you're my main attraction and that ought to count for something."

It did.

CHAPTER 12

Roy Winslow. He had the appearance of a young minister or, perhaps, an attorney fresh out of law school. But that was on the outside. Inside, he had the cold nerves and calculating will of a bounty hunter. He stood on the low porch of San Diego's town hall. Careful to show just the right measure of a grimace from his wound, Roy lifted his arms for silence and the crowd obliged.

"I can't tell the story over and over so I guess I better get it all out at once. First off, I know you're wondering about my opponent for sheriff, Glen Collins. You can rest easy. They're in no danger. I returned two of the killers but one got away. We think he's wounded and shouldn't cause much of a problem. Also, he's on foot and that will make it easy for Glen to capture him. These two, as you all can plainly see, refused to come in peaceably. Hap Hazard, who you all know, was good enough to tie them down for me."

Off to the side, Roy waved at the lean old hunter. In return, Hap spat in the dirt and reined his horse away. He was mad. That was fine. In fact, perfect. Let the old man get his feathers in a ruffle—as long as he stayed out of the way.

"Hap's a little tired but I want you to know I couldn't have done it without his help, or Glen's, or even Maria's.

It was a tragedy and I want you to know when I become sheriff, you good folks won't need to worry about this kind of thing."

He glanced over at his brother Josh, who had his arms folded across his chest. There was something to his expression that didn't bode well. Roy decided to send a little plug his way. After all, he thought, even Josh has to be voted into office. "I'll spare you the chilling details of how we done it, it wasn't a thing I enjoyed or that women or children should hear."

There was a low murmur of protest, especially, Roy noted with amusement, from the ladies and kids. But relating the events as they happened wasn't in his plan. Without actually saying anything, he could sense that they believed Roy Winslow was the man they could thank. When Glen Collins returned, no one could say he'd lied. Roy was a master at the subtle art of unspoken suggestion; it worked effectively with a crowd or a woman.

"I'd like to tell you folks more but—" he squinted, bit his lip as though from an awful sudden pain, "but I should get to the doctor before I lose any more blood." His voice quavered weakly, and his audience strained forward anxiously. "I'm just proud, proud as could be to have been able to serve your . . . no, my town, as well as my brother Josh's."

He feigned a stagger, and instantly, a half dozen people jumped up on the porch to support him. Roy let them practically carry him to the doctor's office. Masterfully done, he thought, I shoulda been a Shakespearean actor. Would have made a great Julius Caesar.

Later that evening, with the sweet flush of triumph still coursing through his veins, Roy Winslow settled into an easy chair and helped himself to one of his brother's cigars. He hadn't been able to put off the meeting any longer. He puffed contentedly for a minute and tried to guess what was on Josh's mind. His brother's reception had been, after an initial moment of concern, very cool.

"All right, Josh," he said. "No use of us sitting here glaring at each other. Speak your mind. I want to know what's bothering you. Damned if I can figure it, but you're about the only one in town who ain't treating me like a hero."

Josh Winslow was shorter than his brother and not nearly as handsome, but he had learned to use his voice with surprising effectiveness. He was a shrewd judge of men and he knew finesse wouldn't have any effect on Roy. He cleared his voice and said, "You're not a hero. Not one damn bit. All you are is a slick-talking, trigger-happy kid."

The cigar smoke in Roy's mouth went bad. He coughed, and before he could protest, Josh drove in harder. "I spoke to Hap Hazard. The story he tells is one hell of a lot different than your posturing oratory at the town hall."

"Not true! Goddamnit, Josh, I didn't lie."

"Of course not! That's what really burns me up. Your cleverness and the fact that you killed a man on that beach that had surrendered!"

"I didn't know that!" Roy was on his feet. He stood before his older brother like a kid before a schoolteacher awaiting punishment. Josh was always right; he was the only man alive Roy was in awe of. "Josh, I'm your brother. You have to believe me."

Josh removed his glasses, ran his fingers through his prematurely graying hair. "Sit down, Roy," he said wearily. "We've got some decisions to make."

He obeyed. Once seated, he was barely able to find his voice. "Decisions?"

"What are we going to do with you?"

"Huh?"

"Your future," Josh said loudly. "What about it?"

Roy blinked. "Well," he stammered, "I'm going to become sheriff and settle down. I kind of favor that Señorita Silvas. Course she . . ."

"No!" Josh blurted. "Forget about being sheriff or marrying the Silvas girl."

"What!" Roy exclaimed, bounding out of his chair. He rushed over to the liquor cabinet. His hands felt clumsy and he spilled whiskey as he poured. He couldn't believe his brother. Roy emptied his glass and poured another before turning around. He had to get control.

"Take it easy," Josh said, his voice softening. "Remember, I'm your brother and I'm on your side."

Roy laughed bitterly. "That's a relief. For a moment, I thought I was speaking to an enemy like Glen Collins."

"Collins isn't your enemy. He's a good man and he'll make a fine sheriff. He'll also marry Maria Silvas and that was decided long before you rode into San Diego."

"I don't believe it! You saw those folks earlier. They'll elect me sure and then Collins is leaving this town. Maria wouldn't go with him; she'll come running to me."

"You're not listening, Roy! I have an offer that will make you change your thinking in a hurry. The Exchange Hotel is the best in town. Eighteen rooms, a dining hall and a bar in the basement." Josh leaned forward with anticipation. "I have offered to buy it, Roy, for twelve thousand, cash. And that includes the stock! Say the word and it's ours! You run it and I'll give you a salary and a partnership. How about it?"

Roy laughed outright. He couldn't help it. "Big profit maker I suppose?"

"Of course it will be! You must have noticed it yourself. Grand old building! I've admired it since the first night I arrived in San Diego. That's where I stayed. The books say it's barely breaking even but that's due to poor management. In a couple years, after we plow some profit back into restoration, we'll make bunches of money. Hell, being a mayor or sheriff is great and I'm proud. But sooner or later we all get turned out of public office and then what?"

"I don't know," Roy said dryly. "You tell me."

"Then nothing," Josh said. "You start over from scratch. Well, I'm saying we can build a future for ourselves around that hotel. Down toward San Diego Bay there's construction going on, a whole settlement they call New Town. Being promoted by a man named Horton who's investing barrelfuls of money. My plan is to buy a business lot there, and after a couple years, if New Town flourishes, we'll build another hotel. Keep expanding. That's the way to make money!"

"That's the way, huh?" Roy asked, feeling a coldness creeping up in his stomach that the whiskey couldn't combat.

"Sure it is! You listen to me. I'm a banker and I've watched how money is made in this town. I've worked hard to get where I am but it's nothing compared to what we can do together."

Roy shook his head sadly. He knew that what he had to say was going to wound Josh, and he wished there were some other path he could take. But it wasn't in the cards and he had to get through to Josh. He'd let his brother say too much already.

"Josh, how about a drink?"

"No thanks. It upsets my stomach."

"Sorry about that," Roy said. "I think I'll have another big one for both of us. 'Cause you see, I'd really like to go into partners with you but the thought of running a hotel upsets *my* stomach. In fact, it makes me sick!"

Josh groaned. The light snuffed out of his eyes. He lowered his head and stared at his hands. "Forgive me, brother, but right now, I don't want money. I want to be this town's first sheriff and I aim to have Maria Silvas for my bride."

Josh leaned forward, his face cupped in his hands. His voice was almost inaudible. "I'll oppose you," he whispered. "Starting tomorrow morning I'll tell everyone I meet what really happened on that beach. I don't want to do it but . . ."

Roy slammed his glass down hard. "Then why? Why the hell don't you mind your own business?"

"Because . . . because I know you! If you become sheriff you'll be dead within a year. Either you'll gun some innocent man down and hang, or someone will hate your guts enough to gun you down from behind. You're not diplomatic or cautious. You act without thinking first —like on the beach. I won't have an innocent man's death or my own brother's on my conscience. So," he ended, "I'll oppose you."

"The hell with your conscience!" Roy said bitterly. "I've made it through life this far without your help. I can make my own decisions." He headed for the door.

"Roy, wait!" Josh pleaded.

Roy hesitated, bowed his head in sadness. "There's nothing to wait for. Nothing to say. I'll be packing my things and moving over to the Exchange Hotel tonight. Tell me, Josh. What room did you stay in?"

"Huh?"

"Your room number! The one you had when you first came to this town."

"Number fourteen. Overlooks San Diego Avenue."

"Thanks," Roy said dully. "If it was a good beginning for you, maybe some luck will also come my way. Kinda obvious I'm going to have to make my own breaks. So long, brother."

On his way to the hotel, Roy tried to find an answer to

his problem. He'd never wanted anything in his life as much as being sheriff and winning the beautiful Maria Silvas. Josh was smart, but he'd been dead wrong in his assessment. Roy figured it was time he stood up and showed the mayor that his brother could make it alone. There was only one thing that stood in his way—Glen Collins.

Thinking hard, Roy stopped on the boardwalk. Unless he eliminated Collins, that overgrown blacksmith was going to cash in on everything. Roy's natural pride revolted. But even so, he was smart enough to realize he couldn't kill the man. That would be too much and both Maria and the citizens would turn against him. So, the only solution was to force a showdown and cripple his opponent. That wouldn't be too hard. Not really. Roy knew he was fast enough to get off at least one bullet before Collins cleared leather, probably two. Maybe one for each leg.

The important thing was that it would have to be witnessed and in self-defense. When the blacksmith heard about his town hall speech, he'd be furious. But angry enough to draw? Maybe not. What then? Roy started walking. He'd think of something, and of that, there was no doubt.

The sun was going down the following day when Glen and Maria returned. On the way back she told him much about Juan Francisco and her childhood he hadn't known. The nearer they'd come to San Diego, the more they'd seemed to draw together. There'd be a funeral tomorrow or the day after. It was going to be hard on her but, after what they'd been through together these past forty hours, he knew she'd endure the sorrow with her head high. Maria was a hell of a woman; she'd be all right.

For his own part, Glen couldn't help thinking about the

election. It was just three days away and he knew Roy Winslow would be out pumping hands and slapping backs. If Roy won, Glen wasn't sure what he'd do. Without the sheriff's pay, he and Maria would have a hard time scrambling to make ends meet. But, somehow, they'd do it. Glen realized he'd been a fool to wait so long. If nothing else, Roy had taught him that lesson.

They said good-by quickly and Glen galloped over to the Blackhawk Livery. Hap Hazard was waiting to meet him. In less than ten minutes, Glen went hunting Roy Winslow. He didn't even wait for Hap; cold fury pushed him down the street at almost a run. Winslow had gone too far this time. Glen figured it was time to set the record straight—once and for all.

The saloon business always did well in San Diego. When Glen barged through the swinging front doors of the Blue Beard at least a dozen men twisted around. For a moment, he squinted through the smoke and dimness. Several customers came at him with outstretched hands offered in congratulations, but Glen pushed by. He'd located Roy Winslow playing cards near the back wall. Glen bulled his way across the room, kicking over chairs in his way. By the time he reached the poker table, the entire saloon crowd could have heard a match strike and would have thought it uncommonly loud.

"Stand up, Winslow!"

Roy placed his cards facedown on the table. He cocked his head sideways toward another player and said, "That sounded like an order. Did it sound like one to you?"

In answer the man kicked back his chair and the other players scrambled to get out of the way.

Roy shook his head and grinned ruefully. "Damnit Collins, you come in at just the wrong time. I had three of a kind and was going for fourth. I'd have won that pot."

"I said stand up. Then I want you to tell this who'

room about your part of the manhunt. Hap told me you changed a few things around. I think it's time you set the record straight."

Up front, the bat-wing doors creaked and Glen knew Hap was behind him. He saw Roy's eyes narrow and guessed Hap was carrying his rifle. Without taking his eyes off Roy, Glen said, "Stay out of this. It's between Winslow and me. I'll brook no interference."

Roy smiled and slowly came to his feet. "You look kind of tired, my friend," he said, loud enough for the room to hear. "What's the matter? Maria Silvas wear you down last night?"

The effect on Glen was probably all Roy hoped and more. Glen blinked, his breathing quickened and his hand lowered over his gun. Gone was any idea of avoiding a gunfight. He knew he couldn't match Winslow's speed but he had to try. "Draw," he said quietly.

"After you, blacksmith. You're the one that's forcing the play. I want that clear to everyone."

A Sharps buffalo rifle, when cocked, makes a very loud and ominous CLICK. It is unmistakable. "You draw, Winslow, first or second doesn't make a damn bit of difference to me. 'Cause I'll put a hole in you big enough for a crow to fly through."

Roy's mouth twitched. He wet his lips and jerked his eyes back to Glen. "Is this how it works?" he demanded. "You can't fight your own battles without the old man? Well," he swallowed, "if he shoots, it will be murder and he'll hang!"

"Hap," Glen said, "put the rifle away."

"Sorry, boy, but I can't do that. You're like my son and I'd rather dance in a noose than let him have his way."

Hap was somewhere behind him but Glen could tell by his voice the old man wasn't bluffing. On rare occasions, he could be as stubborn as the mule he sometimes favored to ride. Glen's shoulders slumped. They were at an impasse. He thought a minute. "Why don't we settle this with our fists. Loser rides out of town."

Roy chuckled softly. He gently patted his side. "Can't do that. I've got a wound. Remember?" He stared down at the card table for a moment, his brows furrowed in concentration. "You know, there are a lot of interesting ways men fight and kill each other. Myself, I always kind of admired sword fighting. But, in my condition, I'm no match for your strength and we'd probably wind up hacking each other into little pieces. Women wouldn't love me if I was say, missing an ear. Nope, that could be real messy."

"Then let's stick to guns," Glen said.

"Well damned if I wouldn't like to. But Josh and Maria would never forgive me. They and everyone else in San Diego knows I'm better than you. But there might be another way to make a fair fight out of it."

"Make it easy on yourself."

"All right," Roy said evenly. "I once saw two Mexicans go at it with knives. But it wasn't any kind of fight I ever saw before." Roy swallowed loudly, his eyes went half shut. "No, I never seen anything like it in my life and I'll never forget. It was just outside of Juárez and they were fighting over a woman. That's generally about all they do fight over."

"Get on with the story," Glen growled.

"Well, they were just poor people and neither one owned a gun. Like as not they'd never even used one. But they both had knives. Only trouble was, one of 'em had a crippled leg and most everyone figured, since he was also pretty runty, it wouldn't be fair. Them folks like to bet on most every kind of thing. Nobody would take even long odds on the runt."

"Winslow, this better be leading up to something fast," Glen said.

"It is. Believe me it is. The upshot of it all was that they put blindfolds on them both. Then they led them down into a gulley and turned them loose. The odds were almost even and we all sat on the bank betting. It was quite a show."

"Then you suggest blindfolds and knives?"

"Uh-uh. They're as bad as swords. What I'm proposing is that we shoot it out in the dark. Say in your big ole livery barn with the front and back doors locked tight. Yes, sir," he said. "We wait until tonight and go in from the front and back with just six bullets apiece. Winner is the one who walks out."

Glen chewed it over. The idea was crazy but he knew Roy was serious. He desperately wanted to make it a fair fight. Probably not because of honor but for Maria. Why not, Glen decided. "Just one thing," he said.

"What's that?"

"Seems I'll have the advantage because I know my surroundings in there better than you."

"I thought of that," Roy drawled. "But on the other hand I am better with a gun and a smaller target. I'd say it all evens out."

"Then let's do it," Glen said. "I'll meet you in front of my place at dusk."

Roy offered his hand and Glen shook it. Their eyes locked and Glen couldn't help wishing it might have been settled some other way. The heat was out of him, and as he saw Roy nod, he had a feeling Winslow was already beginning to regret the challenge. Glen fished for something he could say.

But before he had a chance, Roy released his grip and addressed the onlookers. "You all heard us," he said loudly. "So if anyone wants to start betting, I've got a hundred dollars says I come out of there alive tonight. Who wants to cover my bet."

Glen ducked away and stomped for the door. On his way out, he saw a couple men reach into their pockets for money. But most didn't. A wry grin crossed his lips. He was still the underdog.

CHAPTER 13

It was almost sundown and Glen stood in the dim livery barn and waited. He'd emptied the stalls and led each horse to the outside corral for safety. Now, there was nothing left to do until Roy Winslow appeared. In the meantime, he would use his time well.

Several years earlier when he'd bought the Blackhawk Livery, it had been a rough shell of a building one hundred feet square. He erected the hayloft himself and six stalls along the east wall. Each stall was made out of heavy planks and about chest high. They covered almost a third of the ground floor. The rest of the space was undivided but not uncluttered. The skeletons of no less than four wagons stood in various stages of repair. Buying broken wagons and fixing them for resale was one of the ways he made his living. To the front of the barn and right behind the heavy doors stood his anvil and forge. There were several barrels of used, rusting horseshoes. Stacked against the wall was a box of iron cut and ready to be shaped and forged. A water barrel for dousing the shoes stood near the wall. Besides the clutter of wagons and his work area, there was also a section devoted to the storage of saddles and riding equipment.

Glen surveyed everything with measured care. It wasn't as though he'd have the total advantage of familiarity. Up until Roy's return with Bill Singleton and Rafe Dockins, he'd kept his horse in the first stall. Roy knew the layout.

"Glen?"

He twisted around and saw her framed in the doorway. She stood there waiting for him. Glen found he couldn't move. Across the distance of thirty feet he felt as though a lifetime separated them.

"Maria," he finally said, his voice subdued. "Go home. I'll be along later."

She began to walk toward him and he felt himself powerless to stop her. He opened his arms and she ran the last few steps to bury her face against his chest. He felt her shaking.

"Maria, go back to your house. I know why you've come and what you want me to do. I . . . I'm sorry. I can't do it and I don't want you to ask. Do you understand?"

Her head rubbed up and down against his chest and she grew still.

"Then go home," he repeated. "I'll be along in a while."

She ducked her head and ran. And as she passed through the door, Glen's stomach tightened. He saw Roy Winslow.

Roy stepped inside. Glen couldn't see his face because of the gloom but the voice was unmistakable and full of contempt. "That was damned touching, Collins. If you had any sense at all you'd run for it. I'm giving you one final chance."

Suddenly, Glen wanted nothing more than to settle things once and for all. No more talk, no more threatening. In answer, he turned his back and strode to the big rear doors. He grabbed one, then the other and slammed them shut. "Six bullets ought to be enough," he said. "You wouldn't be packing a hideout, would you?"

Roy brayed with laughter. It echoed in the darkness and set Glen's teeth on edge. "Hell no," he swore. "I've given you every advantage up to this point. Why should I cheat now?"

"Beats me."

The light was almost gone behind Roy and only the silhouette remained. Glen saw him unbuckle his cartridge belt and holster and toss them outside. The gun remained in his hand. "Have you seen the crowds outside?"

The question caught Glen off-balance. "No," he said at last.

"You should have looked. It's almost like with those two Mexicans I told you about. There's a lot of betting going on." A dry chuckle. "You're long odds."

Glen shifted his weight, his hand on his gun butt. "Close the doors and let's get the show started."

But Roy didn't move. He seemed to want to talk. Perhaps, Glen thought, to see if I'll lose my nerve.

"Just between us, Collins. I did almost bring a derringer. But I won't need it for you. Besides, those folks out there might notice the difference in sound and start adding things up."

"Close the door!" Glen was surprised at the loudness of his voice. He was getting rattled. His nerves tightened and tore like strands of barbed wire. *Get ahold of yourself!*

"You know, of all those people outside, only two wanted to talk me out of this showdown. Maria and Josh. That kinda tells you something about folks, doesn't it?" He twisted around and pulled the first door shut. The barn was almost black. Roy was no more than a shadow.

The second door began to close. "Well, Collins, good luck," the voice said. "In a way I'm real sorry it has to end like this. If it wasn't that we both fancied Maria and being sheriff, I think I might even have liked you."

The door was almost to the wall. It stopped for a last second.

"Oh yeah, I wanted to say I felt rotten about the *contradanza*. But, as they say, 'All's fair in love and war.'"

The barn door slammed shut like a coffin lid. Glen ducked sideways and a shot boomed. He heard the bullet WHAP into wood close by and saw the muzzle flash. He pumped a shot and a split second later got return fire. The bullet passed so close Glen swore he could feel its heat.

He crouched on his heels and tried to listen but the enclosed gunfire seemed to have deadened his ears. Then he heard the loud pounding of Roy's boots. There was a crash and grunt. Then more steps. Glen stared so hard his eyes ached. He felt his heart pounding in his chest. His gun tracked an imaginary ghost and he fired. There was a THUD and Glen blinked. Had he scored?

Two blasts of Roy's weapon answered the question. The first bullet screamed over his head and the second kicked his hat off. Glen rolled sideways and hugged the dirt trying to organize his thoughts. Stay low! he told himself. That was why Roy had missed. It was the only reason he was still alive! Glen hugged the ground, his body drenched in sweat. He didn't know where Roy was. Only that the man was close.

"Hey, Collins? You still alive?"

The voice was to his left. It sounded like a shout it was so close. Glen fired at the sound and rolled sideways. But not fast enough. Roy wasn't stupid. He shot low and Glen felt the bullet dig into his leg. An involuntary gasp burst from his lips. He punched another shot off and dove backward. Then he scrambled on his hands and knees. He had to get to cover. He rolled behind the end stall and lay still. He wiped his sleeve across his face and reached down and gripped his leg. In the blackness he couldn' tell how bad he'd been hit but his fingers explored the wound and he knew it wasn't serious. Yet it was. The numbness was spreading and Glen worried that it would slow him down. He had to be able to move fast.

"Hey Collins! I know you're hiding behind the stalls. And I know you're hit. Are you dying?"

Glen had to smile; the question was so hopeful. It was almost a full minute before Roy spoke again and the voice was closer. He was moving down the stalls. Glen guessed he wasn't more than three away. "You better answer me. 'Cause if you're dying I'll call it off. I could go get Maria for you. That'd be nice. Wouldn't you like to die in her arms, Collins?"

Glen climbed to his feet and tested the leg. It was numb and seemed apart but it held his weight. How many bullets did Winslow have left? Glen tried to count; he did it twice before he was convinced Roy had one bullet left. But did that matter? Could he really take the chance that Roy hadn't had a pistol stuffed under his shirt? He'd been mighty free with his bullets. Glen forgot about counting; he'd be a fool to assume Roy was playing the rules.

"Listen," Roy said, his voice calm and persuasive. "I heard you move so I know you're alive. But you need a doctor, right? Otherwise, you might bleed to death. Throw your pistol at the far wall. I'll know by the sound if it's a gun and I'll let you live. Send for a doctor."

There was a long silence and when Roy spoke again, the arrogance and mocking were gone. "Glen," he said quietly, "I'll give you five seconds and then I'm coming. I never shot a defenseless man and I don't want to now. But you ain't talking and I can't take the chance. I'm starting my count. Throw your gun."

He listened to the count as he moved. The floor was dirt and he faded away from the stalls groping until his fingers touched a wagon. He fumbled in the darkness, searching for something, anything, to grab and throw. Yes it was an old trick but he wasn't feeling very clever. Besides, Roy's nerves were as raw as his own. He might fire instinctively and if he did, Glen would have him pinpointed.

"Five." The count ended and Glen heard the whisper steps. His fingers touched something and he tightened his grip on a discarded wooden brake shoe. Glen raised his arm and hurled the object toward the last stall.

The reaction was instantaneous. A flash of gunpowder spewed from Roy's gun and there was a crashing sound. Glen shot and heard a yell. He charged forward, misjudged the stall and crashed into the fence. His bad leg went out from under him and he fell.

Roy was inside the stall! Glen raised his gun and poked it forward. He started to pull the trigger. He couldn't know exactly how Roy lay but the stall wasn't that big. He had two bullets left.

"Glen! I'm hit!"

He eased off on the trigger. His eyes stared so hard into the inky darkness he felt like they were going to pop out of his head.

"Glen, help me!" The voice was ragged. Panicky.

Glen waited, frozen with uncertainty. If Roy has another gun and I go in there, he thought, I'm dead. But what if the man *was* dying? Glen edged aside until his body was out of the stall's entrance. For the first time, he spoke and his voice sounded like a rusty gate-hinge. "Roy, you need help?"

There was a moment's silence then, "Yeah." So softly i couldn't have been heard more than a few feet away.

Glen stood and, with his gun pointed at the place he judged Roy to be, he hobbled inside. His finger increase the pressure on the trigger. If Roy was setting him up

Glen wanted it certain he'd at least get off one shot and that would be enough.

There was no answering gunfire. Glen stepped closer and his foot touched Roy's boot. "How bad are you hit?"

"Bad enough," Roy gritted.

"I'll find a lamp," Glen said. Roy was out of bullets. If he'd had an extra gun he would have used it by now. Glen holstered his weapon and reached out, groping for the stall door.

Roy hit him in the back with a tackle that almost snapped Glen's spine. They both struck the floor and a fist slammed down and glanced off Glen's forehead. Glen swung blindly and missed everything. Roy was a wild man. And though he lacked Glen's size, his punches were cat-quick and hard. Roy was on top and his knuckles seemed accurate enough to have night eyes.

Glen's fingers gripped Roy's shirt and he heaved him off. Then he rolled over onto his knees and felt the air shift as Roy's punch swept by his head. Glen lunged out and managed to wrap an arm around Roy's neck. He put all his strength into the hold and Roy began to gag. Glen yanked out his gun and shoved the barrel into Winslow's ear. The man froze.

"I can't miss now," Glen panted. He eased up on the choke hold and heard Roy's sharp intake of breath.

"Then shoot, damn you! I won't beg. You won fair. Don't play with me, Collins."

Glen felt the man tense under his arm and his Adam's apple bob. Winslow was ready to die.

"I thought you'd have another gun," Glen said. "Why didn't you?"

A laugh rattled in Roy's throat. "I didn't think you'd have one so . . . so I didn't. I guess that makes me a worse fool than you are."

Glen considered about that for a minute. And during

that time, the pressure on his trigger finger eased. "You aren't going to die," he said finally. "But you'll have to go to jail. I guess we both will."

"Maybe you," Roy said tightly, "but not me. I've thought about this and I ain't going to no jail again. You'd better pull that trigger. I swear you'll have to kill me first!"

"You're bluffing. Don't force me to do this." Glen's voice pleaded. "I don't want to kill you. Stop talking crazy."

"Crazy for you!" Roy gasped. "But I'm wanted in Arizona and Mexico. The word will get out and I'll have a federal officer putting cuffs on me. I would rot in prison!"

"What did you do?" Glen asked, almost afraid to hear the answer.

"I killed men," came the reply. "And every one of 'em was a woman beater. I don't regret a one of 'em. But each time I stepped between a man and his wife. So, like I said, you might as well pull the trigger.'

"You really mean that, don't you?" Glen asked wearily. He pressed the gun hard against Roy's skull.

"I never meant anything more in my life," the voice whispered.

Glen swallowed dryly. "O.K.," he sighed. "It's your choice. Josh will see your funeral is the best."

CHAPTER 14

Glen worked fast. He located a lantern and struck a match, careful to keep the wick burning low. Next, he found a clean horse blanket and respectfully draped the body. Satisfied, he bent down and picked Roy up and staggered toward the barn doors. He had expected a handful of the curious, but when he emerged from Blackhawk Livery, he blinked in amazement. A sea of onlookers awaited the outcome. They held hundreds of lanterns aloft and the street was as bright as day.

With his appearance, people stopped talking in midsentence and there was hushed silence. All eyes were on him and they expected something. What, he wasn't sure. Glen surveyed them, his eyes traveled from one face to another. Later, he knew, he would feel different about these citizens; but right at that moment, he felt utter contempt.

"I am sorry you folks couldn't see the whole show," he snapped icily. Inside, a voice told him to stop. Maybe they were just acting out of concern. True, some had betted on the outcome. But perhaps that was normal. The bitterness eased inside.

He searched for his next words. "What I regret the most is that this man and I couldn't settle our differences without guns. He fought fair and by the rules. There's been way too much killing these past few weeks. I'm as much to blame as anyone. As sheriff, I'm going to make it my job to keep the peace as long as it's possible. You all have my word on that. It's a promise."

Maria stepped out from the ring of onlookers. She held a lantern and he followed her through the people. Just as they were about past everyone, Josh Winslow blocked their path. This was the one person Glen had dreaded facing.

He rooted his feet to the ground not knowing what to expect. If the mayor had spit in his face or started cursing him, Glen wouldn't have been overly surprised. But Josh did neither. There were tears in his eyes and the muscles in his face moved his skin around like a can of fishing worms. He raised his hands imploringly, then dropped them to his side. Glen saw the man's wife pull at his coat sleeve but Josh didn't seem to notice.

Finally the mayor reached out and started to fold back the covering from Roy's face. Glen stepped back, looked into the glazed eyes and said, "Don't do it. It was dark and . . . I don't want you to see his face."

Josh blinked and for the first time, Glen had the impression that the mayor really saw him and understood. The man nodded to himself and left.

The body in his arms was growing very heavy. Glen started walking again, every step sent fire through the leg. Several hands reached out to help but he shook them away.

The mortician's office wasn't far and Glen could see the man waiting for his business. He wore a black derby only when at work. Glen remembered him as an officious and sanctimonious individual who constantly made reference to the Bible. He would have been a successful preacher except that he lacked a smile and seemed devoid o warmth. The mortician had few friends; perhaps he felt it beneath his profession to form personal attachments.

Glen managed to gain the boardwalk but just barely. The mortician made a sweeping gesture and said, "Just come inside and place the deceased on the table. I'll handle everything."

"Your best coffin," Glen said. "Wheel it out and let's put the body inside."

"Sir! The deceased must be prepared."

Glen motioned Maria to leave. When she was outside, he stepped up very close to the man and said, "He goes in now. I shot him in the face!"

For a person used to corpses, the mortician's reaction was almost violent. His gray skin drew back from the corners of his mouth in shock. "In the face?" he whispered.

"That's right, and no man should see the result. That's why I insist the coffin is sealed now. Do you understand?"

He nodded and disappeared into the back room. Glen heard movement and a minute later he wheeled out a coffin. "The burial will have to be immediate. First thing tomorrow I should think. What the Lord giveth, the Lord hath taken away from us." Then he added. "It's a shame he was taken away so . . . so messily."

Glen didn't comment. He helped the mortician lift the body and settle it into place. Then they shut the lid and fastened it down.

Glen leaned heavily against the table. The coffin was beautiful. Solid mahogany wood polished and glossy. The fittings were brass and along the side were red velvet pull ropes. Roy would be proud and his brother would be poorer.

"May he rest in peace," the mortician's voice quavered. A thin hand patted Glen's shoulder. "Don't feel too badly about your own part in this, Mr. Collins. Perhaps it was

His design and you were merely His obedient servant. God works in strange ways."

He isn't the only one, Glen thought, hobbling toward the door. Outside, he took Maria's arm and they headed for the doctor's office.

Dr. John Raymond was the antithesis of the mortician. He was young and wasted little time in patching Glen's leg. "A flesh wound," he said. "The bullet passed through cleanly but it's going to hurt damn bad the first week. Stop by every afternoon until I'm sure it's healing cleanly. In the meantime, keep your weight off the leg."

"That's impossible, Doctor. I can't set around."

The doctor snorted and scratched his jaw. "Well," he said finally, "I'll give you a crutch to lean on. Just try and keep the weight off, all right?"

"Sure." He waited until the doctor brought the crutch, then headed for the door. He was going to have to get used to the thing. He kept tripping on the floor end.

With Maria steadying him, Glen traversed the town and at last reached the Blackhawk. They'd spoken very few words on the way over and before she left he said, "Maria, I'd like you to stay a few minutes. There are some things we should settle."

"What's there to settle?" she whispered. "I should pray in thanks that you are alive."

"And Roy Winslow?"

She dipped her head. "I'll pray he's at peace."

Glen lifted her chin until their eyes met. "You liked him very much, didn't you?"

"Yes," she admitted. "But I loved you."

"That's what I wanted to hear," he said. "Before you go, I want to know what you liked most about Roy. Perhaps I can be some of those things and you'll love me even more."

She smiled sadly. "Roy has already given you some of

those things. He taught you how to dress for a fiesta and . . ."

"And how not to do the *contradanza*," Glen said with a grin.

"Yes. I suspected as much. But think about it, Glen, and you will agree he brought us closer together than ever before. And one final thing."

"What's that?"

"I will always remember the night I needed help and he ran to save your life."

"I couldn't forget that myself," he said quietly.

"Then how?" She bit off the question and it hung in the air between them.

Glen looked down at the dirt. His lips tightened thoughtfully and he said, "He isn't dead, Maria."

"What!" Disbelief spread across her face. "Glen I saw him. We all did! And the blood."

"My blood smeared on a dangling arm. He's alive."

She jumped forward and grabbed him by the neck kissing his face. Glen tottered on the crutch, swiveled around, and fell with her in his arms.

"That is wonderful!"

Glen rolled over and propped himself up on one elbow. "Now that you know," he chuckled, "do you want to help set him free?"

"Yes! But then what?" She paused and frowned. "The funeral and everything. What . . ."

"The funeral will go ahead as planned. But tonight, Roy will ride away a free man. He'll take a new name and make a fresh start. I made him swear to leave married women alone as long as he lives."

"Where is he going?"

"San Francisco, he thinks. He said something about boarding a sailing ship and seeing the world."

Maria beamed and scrambled to her feet. She helped Glen stand. "Come. We must hurry."

"Take it easy. I told him I'd wait a couple hours until I was certain the town was asleep."

"We can't. Don't you know coffins are airtight? He could suffocate!"

"Oh no," Glen breathed. He broke into a hobble. "I'll tell Hap to get a horse saddled. Now!"

Minutes later they were moving toward San Diego Avenue. They passed down the back streets and cut into the alley behind the mortician's office. The door was unlocked and they wasted no time getting inside.

For a split second, he and Maria's eyes met, both afraid of what they might discover. Glen struck a match and his fingers shook, casting dancing shadows on the funeral parlor wall. Then, he shot the bolts and swung open the lid. "Roy!"

Roy jackknifed erect and Maria screamed.

"I am the ghost of the dead," he intoned, staring straight ahead. "I have risen to haunt you!"

Maria staggered back, her hand flying to her mouth. Glen's finger burned and the match went out. Instinctively, he shoved Roy down and started to slam the coffin lid.

"Wait! Wait!" Roy cried. "I was only kidding!" Roy batted the lid aside and hopped from the casket. And in the darkness, all three began to laugh.

True to his word, Roy Winslow climbed onto his horse and raced out of San Diego going like the wind—fast and free. The next day they buried the coffin. It seemed amazingly heavy. Probably because Glen managed to dispose of three barrels of rusty horseshoes.

In everyone's opinion, it was about the biggest funeral they had all year. Especially evident was Howard Trimmer and his riders. He amazed everyone because he even took off his stetson during the service.

When it was over and the funeral party had left the hillside cemetery, only three people remained. Josh Winslow stood over the grave and stared down with reddish, swollen eyes. If only he'd been able to reason with his younger brother. Perhaps he never really tried. Maybe he'd been too intent on forcing Roy into something against his nature. Too late now. A tragic mistake.

Some ten feet behind him, Maria Silvas nudged Glen forward. He hobbled up and placed a hand on Winslow's bent shoulders. Glen talked for only a few minutes. As he did, the other seemed to straighten, grow taller. The man who was destined to be the first sheriff turned away and the señorita took his arm.

They were only ten yards down the hillside when they heard a wild squeal of laughter. Glen twisted around on his crutch and saw Josh Winslow's hat sailing up toward the bright, blue San Diego sky.

POWDER RIVER

Gary McCarthy

Utah in the mid-1800s is truly wild, a land still largely untamed by law and settled by only the strongest—and bravest—souls. Few men have the courage to survive. And even fewer women. Despite the odds, Katie remains. A young, single woman, she is determined to raise her child and manage her sheep ranch without the help of any man...though a powerful cattleman, a ranch hand and an Eastern gentleman each have different ideas.

___4408-0 $5.50 US/$6.50 CAN

Dorchester Publishing Co., Inc.
P.O. Box 6640
Wayne, PA 19087-8640

Please add $1.75 for shipping and handling for the first book and $.50 for each book thereafter. NY, NYC, and PA residents, please add appropriate sales tax. No cash, stamps, or C.O.D.s. All orders shipped within 6 weeks via postal service book rate. Canadian orders require $2.00 extra postage and must be paid in U.S. dollars through a U.S. banking facility.

Name_____
Address_____
City_____ State_____ Zip_____
I have enclosed $_____ in payment for the checked book(s).
Payment <u>must</u> accompany all orders. ❏ Please send a free catalog.
CHECK OUT OUR WEBSITE! www.dorchesterpub.com

SODBUSTER

GARY McCARTHY

In the ranching communities of 1870s Wyoming, sodbusters are just about as low on the social scale as farm animals. And it's a life that Zach and Carrie Bennett are determined to escape. Once they hit the trail to Texas, though, they realize just how dangerous their escape will be. Their incredible journey through the lawless Wild West will show them human nature at its most base . . . and unveil a strength and a capacity for violence the brother and sister never believed possible in themselves.

__4467-6 $4.50 US/$5.50 CAN

Dorchester Publishing Co., Inc.
P.O. Box 6640
Wayne, PA 19087-8640

Please add $1.75 for shipping and handling for the first book and $.50 for each book thereafter. NY, NYC, and PA residents, please add appropriate sales tax. No cash, stamps, or C.O.D.s. All orders shipped within 6 weeks via postal service book rate. Canadian orders require $2.00 extra postage and must be paid in U.S. dollars through a U.S. banking facility.

Name_____
Address_____
City_____State_____Zip_____
I have enclosed $_____ in payment for the checked book(s).
Payment <u>must</u> accompany all orders. ❏ Please send a free catalog.

THE MUSTANGERS
GARY McCARTHY

In Nevada in the early 1860s, an increasingly profitable trade is springing up. It is called mustanging—the breaking and selling of rogue horses to the highest bidder. When Pete Sills, an eager apprentice mustanger, signs on at the Cross T Ranch, all he wants is to learn the trade. But as soon as he meets Candy, the ranch owner's daughter, all that changes. Now he wants her. But to win her he first has to capture Sun Dancer, the fabulous palomino that Candy has her heart set on. And that means more trouble for Pete than he can ever imagine... and a lesson about pride and courage that he will never forget.

__4518-4 $3.99 US/$4.99 CAN

Dorchester Publishing Co., Inc.
P.O. Box 6640
Wayne, PA 19087-8640

Please add $1.75 for shipping and handling for the first book and $.50 for each book thereafter. NY, NYC, and PA residents, please add appropriate sales tax. No cash, stamps, or C.O.D.s. All orders shipped within 6 weeks via postal service book rate. Canadian orders require $2.00 extra postage and must be paid in U.S. dollars through a U.S. banking facility.

Name_____
Address_____
City_____ State_____ Zip_____
I have enclosed $_____ in payment for the checked book(s).
Payment <u>must</u> accompany all orders. ❏ Please send a free catalog.
CHECK OUT OUR WEBSITE! www.dorchesterpub.com

BLOOD BROTHERS
GARY McCARTHY

Ben Pope and Rick Kilbane are as different as night and day. A miner's son, Ben is an awkward, earnest kid with no money and lots of hard luck. Rick is the wild, troublemaking son of Ulysses Kilbane, a professional gambler and the fastest gun on Nevada's Comstock Lode. But despite their differences, Ben and Rick have always been best friends and blood brothers. That may all change, though, now that Ben has pinned on a sheriff's badge. That tin star has set the blood brothers down the road to the ultimate showdown—a final test of friendship and loyalty. A test that one of them may not survive.

___4585-0 $3.99 US/$4.99 CAN

Dorchester Publishing Co., Inc.
P.O. Box 6640
Wayne, PA 19087-8640

Please add $1.75 for shipping and handling for the first book and $.50 for each book thereafter. NY, NYC, and PA residents, please add appropriate sales tax. No cash, stamps, or C.O.D.s. All orders shipped within 6 weeks via postal service book rate. Canadian orders require $2.00 extra postage and must be paid in U.S. dollars through a U.S. banking facility.

Name_____
Address_____
City_____State_____Zip_____
I have enclosed $_____ in payment for the checked book(s).
Payment <u>must</u> accompany all orders. ❏ Please send a free catalog.
CHECK OUT OUR WEBSITE! www.dorchesterpub.com

DARK TRAIL
Hiram King

When the War Between the States was finally over, many men returned from battle only to find their homes destroyed and their families scattered to the wind. Bodie Johnson is one of those men. But while some families fled before advancing armies, the Johnson family was packed up like cattle and shipped west—on a slave train. With only that information to go on, Bodie sets out to find whatever remains of his family. And he will do it. Because no matter how vast the West is, no matter what stands in his way, Bodie knows one thing—the Johnsons will survive.

___4418-8 $5.50 US/$6.50 CAN

Dorchester Publishing Co., Inc.
P.O. Box 6640
Wayne, PA 19087-8640

Please add $1.75 for shipping and handling for the first book and $.50 for each book thereafter. NY, NYC, and PA residents, please add appropriate sales tax. No cash, stamps, or C.O.D.s. All orders shipped within 6 weeks via postal service book rate. Canadian orders require $2.00 extra postage and must be paid in U.S. dollars through a U.S. banking facility.

Name_____
Address_____
City_____ State_____ Zip_____
I have enclosed $_____ in payment for the checked book(s).
Payment <u>must</u> accompany all orders. ❑ Please send a free catalog.
CHECK OUT OUR WEBSITE! www.dorchesterpub.com

Last Chance

DEE MARVINE

Mattie Hamil is on a frantic journey west. On her own, with only her grit and determination to see her through, she has to find her charming gambler of a fiancé, and she has to do it fast—before her pregnancy shows. From a steamboat along the Missouri River to the rough-and-tumble post-gold-rush town of Last Chance, Montana, Mattie's trek leads her through danger and sorrow, friendship and joy. But even after she finds her fiancé, no bend in the trail leads to what she expected.

___4475-7 $4.99 US/$5.99 CAN

Dorchester Publishing Co., Inc.
P.O. Box 6640
Wayne, PA 19087-8640

Please add $1.75 for shipping and handling for the first book and $.50 for each book thereafter. NY, NYC, and PA residents, please add appropriate sales tax. No cash, stamps, or C.O.D.s. All orders shipped within 6 weeks via postal service book rate. Canadian orders require $2.00 extra postage and must be paid in U.S. dollars through a U.S. banking facility.

Name_____
Address_____
City_____State_____Zip_____
I have enclosed $_____ in payment for the checked book(s).
Payment <u>must</u> accompany all orders. ❑ Please send a free catalog.
CHECK OUT OUR WEBSITE! www.dorchesterpub.com

ATTENTION WESTERN CUSTOMERS!

SPECIAL TOLL-FREE NUMBER
1-800-481-9191

Call Monday through Friday
**10 a.m. to 9 p.m.
Eastern Time**
*Get a free catalogue,
join the Western Book Club,
and order books using your
Visa, MasterCard,
or Discover®*

*Leisure
Books*

GO ONLINE WITH US AT DORCHESTERPUB.COM

THE CHALLENGE

"Why ain't you wearing a gun?" Chase demanded. He swiveled around to the onlookers. "This man is supposed to be running for sheriff, boys. But he's afraid to pack a six-shooter 'cause he might get shot. Is this the kind you want to elect to keep the peace in San Diego?"

There was a low murmur of voices and shaking of heads. Chase rotated back, his face triumphant. "See," he said. "You ain't fit to be a sheriff. What would you do if somebody called you out and told you to fill your hand or light out of town?"

"I'd be wearing a gun if I was sheriff."

A look of contempt curled Chase's lips. "You're worthless, Collins. You don't want to be sheriff, what you really want is to parade around wearing a badge and hoping that Silvas girl is impressed long enough to bed down with you."

Glen launched himself from the bar and drove forward, knocking over tables in his rush to get to Chase Lawson. At that moment, he was a wild man. He didn't think that Chase might draw his gun and shoot. He didn't think at all.

Other *Leisure* books by Gary McCarthy:
THE GRINGO AMIGO
WIND RIVER
POWDER RIVER
SODBUSTER
THE MUSTANGERS
BLOOD BROTHERS